quaking

To Bill—Thanks for being our Sam.

Special thanks to Patricia Lee Gauch and
Tamra Tuller for teaching me to tie the theads together
and weave a richer story,
and to my children for kissing the manuscript good luck
before mailing.

Patricia Lee Gauch, Editor

PHILOMEL BOOKS
A division of Penguin Young Readers Group. Published by The Penguin Group.
Penguin Group (USA) Inc., 375 Hudson Street, New York, NY 10014, U.S.A.
Penguin Group (Canada), 10 Eglinton Avenue East, Suite 700, Toronto, Ontario, Canada M4P 2Y3
(a division of Pearson Penguin Canada Inc.).
Penguin Books Ltd., 80 Strand, London WC2R 0RL, England.
Penguin Ireland, 25 St. Stephen's Green, Dublin 2, Ireland
(a division of Penguin Books Ltd).
Penguin Group (Australia), 250 Camberwell Road, Camberwell, Victoria 3124, Australia (a division of
Pearson Australia Group Pty Ltd).
Penguin Books India Pvt Ltd., 11 Community Centre, Panchsheel Park,
New Delhi—110 017, India.
Penguin Group (NZ), 67 Apollo Drive, Rosedale, North Shore 0745, Auckland,
New Zealand (a division of Pearson New Zealand Ltd.).
Penguin Books (South Africa) (Pty) Ltd., 24 Sturdee Avenue, Rosebank,
Johannesburg 2196, South Africa.
Penguin Books Ltd, Registered Offices: 80 Strand, London WC2R 0RL, England.

Published simultaneously in Canada. Printed in the United States of America.
The text is set in 12-point Bembo. Design by Semadar Megged.
Library of Congress Cataloging-in-Publication Data
Erskine, Kathryn. Quaking / Kathryn Erskine. p. cm.
Summary: In a Pennsylvania town where anti-war sentiments are treated with contempt and violence, Matt,
a fourteen-year-old girl living with a Quaker family, deals with the demons of her past as she batttles bullies
of the present, eventually learning to trust in others as well as herself.
[1. Patriotism—Fiction. 2. Toleration—Fiction. 3. High schools—Fiction. 4. Schools—Fiction.
5. Quakers—Fiction. 6. Family life—Pennsylvania—Fiction. 7. Self-actualization (Psychology).] I. Title.
PZ7.E7388Qua 2007 [Fic]—dc22 2006034563

ISBN 978-0-399-24774-3
1 3 5 7 9 10 8 6 4 2
First Impression

quaking

KATHRYN ERSKINE

Philomel Books

CHAPTER ONE

Families come in all varieties but with no warranties. I have lived with first cousins twice removed, second cousins once removed, and now a third cousin who is removing herself. I call her Loopy. Because of her large earrings. And because she is insane.

Loopy drives like a ten-year-old car thief on a sugar high. "Don't worry," she says, as we skid across the ice-encrusted Pennsylvania Turnpike, "everything will be fine."

We are driving to my next hostile takeover. I crouch in the back because the front seat implies friendship. It is also the Seat of Death with Loopy behind the wheel. The Loopmobile doubles as her self-storage facility so I pile rolls of toilet paper and a bag of rock salt on top of me for protection.

"I wish I could bring you on my Mission but it's no trip for a girl." Loopy sighs. "Some of the places I'm going, they don't even want to *hear* about Jesus." She shakes her head and her earrings do loop-de-loops.

Loopy is taking Jesus on the road, whether He wants to go or not, and apparently there is not room for all three of us. I tell Him that being nailed to a cross would be preferable to riding with Loopy but I am sure He does not hear me. He never does.

"You need some TLC, sugar."

TLC is not "Tender Loving Care" in Loopy-speak. It stands for "The Love of Christ."

Give me an Almighty Break. Like most of my born-again relatives, Loopy feels more at home with Jesus than with me. But I do not care for them, anyway. Nor do I care for the pseudo-religious relatives, who could only get five of the Ten Commandments right on a pop quiz—six, if they said, "Jesus Christ, I always forget these!" and then remembered the one about not taking God's name in vain. The nonreligious cousins, who do not even pretend to be sacred, are more my style. Except they get fed up with me faster because there is no Jesus screaming at them to be nice to their enemies.

Loopy shakes her earrings. "What's going on with you, Matt? You're a sweet girl, and so smart, too."

According to most, it is my mouth that is smart. And occasionally my ass.

Loopy sighs. "I finally found a second cousin of mine, but you need to make it work, Matt. This is the end of the line for you."

I glare at the rearview mirror.

"They're ... um ... different but ... really religious." Her earrings spin.

Oh, God. It is a cult. I just know it.

"They're Quakers."

Quakers? Excuse me? I thought Quakers were extinct. Or maybe that was Shakers. It was one of those trembling-type religions. Who can keep up? I am not even sure it is a religion. Maybe it is a commune. Or a disease. Oh, God, is there no one else?

"You'll love these people, honey."

I do not love anyone. I have no feelings. She should know that.

"Give them a chance, okay?"

My stomach acid is eating my internal organs. I must be carsick. I try to open my window, then remember that nothing works in the Loopmobile.

I chew my nails.

"Stop chewing your nails. And spit out any nail bits you have in your mouth."

I have nothing in my mouth. Except wicked words. I shoot my Evil Woman look at the back of her head.

"I saw that!" she says, without turning around.

I hide behind my wall of rock salt and chew my nails some more.

"Their names are Sam and Jessica."

Sam and Jessica? They sound old-fashioned and fairy-tale-ish, like *Little House on the Prairie*. Could it be? I am picturing a farmhouse. Sam is in overalls chopping wood. Jessica is in a long dress and is baking me some apple crisp. It is my favorite dessert but no one has ever baked it for me. I have just enjoyed it by accident because someone else wanted it.

"They'll love you, I'm sure. They're already foster parents for a disabled boy."

My face gets squashed against the window as the Loopmobile spirals its way around an exit ramp. I stare out into the snow and see the spindly trees that have a coating of ice on them, still, hard, and cold. As we drive down a two-lane highway I see the fawn, also frozen, beside a Dumpster, alive but motionless so no one will see her. I understand. It is the only way to survive in the wild. Do not get involved. Do not be noticed.

It is a lesson lost on many. Like Loopy. She makes noise constantly. She is now singing about Making a Joyful Noise unto the Lord. I hope He is finding her yelping joyful because there is no stopping her. The only thing that can interrupt Loopy is herself.

"Oh, look! Here we are!" The Loopmobile takes a sharp left onto a narrow street, heaves over a curb, and jolts to a halt.

I think I might heave, too. My hands and feet are icy cold. I stare at my fingernails, or what is left of them.

Loopy pulls me out of the backseat. I watch the toilet paper and rock salt swallow my niche. I take a breath of the arctic blast, and shards of ice pierce my throat and eyes. I shiver convulsively and drop my backpack in the snow.

Loopy drags me up a path, but not to a farmhouse. Casa Quaker is an ugly, gray, two-story duplex. A huge rainbow flag with giant white letters on it hangs from the roof all the way down to the top of one of the front doors.

"I think that's a peace flag," Loopy says. "You know how Quakers are into peace."

No, actually, I know nothing about Quakers. Besides, the letters on the flag spell PACE. Either they need to buy a vowel or Sam and Jessica are advertising their last name. And they are overly enamored of it.

The door under the PACE flag opens and Loopy shoves me from behind. "Here she is!"

I am definitely not in *Little House on the Prairie*. These

people wear jeans, although you could fit two Jessicas into one pair of Sam's jeans. She is skinny and pinch-faced. Her brown magazine-model hair has a few streaks of gray. I wish I had magazine-model hair. Instead, I have frizz. Sometimes it frizzes out horizontally so I look like a tetrahedron head. But that is better than a tetrahedron body, like Sam's. If he were a handyman, he would be the crack-showing kind.

Loopy pokes my ribs and hisses, "Say hello!"

I open my mouth but the words, if there are any, are frozen.

CHAPTER TWO

My alarm goes off. I do not want to get up. But it is not worth hearing the concerned voices asking me why I am not getting up. So I do. And then I stumble. I believe the stupid, garage-sale sofa bed trips me up on purpose. Every morning. It might have something to do with the fact that there are only six inches between the bed and the wall so it is hard, even for me, to squeeze through. I swear, loudly.

"Mattie! Are you all right?" It is Jessica, shouting her concerned-mother voice up the stairs.

I stomp around while I get dressed to let her know I have survived the attack of the sofa bed again.

I trudge down the worn brown-carpeted steps to the kitchen. I wonder what is for breakfast. I hate the smell of eggs. Especially first thing in the morning. And especially mixed with coffee.

"Eggs?" says Jessica. "Coffee?"

I shake my head, but just barely, so as not to actually barf.

"What can I get for you, then?"

I sigh. I can feel some words coming on. They are not

friendly ones. Shouldn't they be eating oatmeal? Quaker Oats? Isn't that the Quaker national dish?

Sam turns around from his ancient computer in the corner. The little swivel stool screams under his weight, cringing and sighing when he stands up. His big round face is beaming like a kindergarten drawing of the sun.

"Good morning, Mattie! Looks like it's going to be a great day for your first appearance at Franklin High." He picks up his coffee from the table and sniffs it like he is going to snort it through his nose.

I stare past him through the window at the Pittsburgh Steelers "Super Bowl Champs" thermometer, the light from the kitchen illuminating it enough to see that the dial is way to the left on the dashing black football helmet.

"It is four frigging degrees," I say, the first words I have spoken to them since I moved in two days ago. It is important for the first words to be harsh. So they know not to get involved. It is for their own good.

Sam gapes at me and spills steaming coffee down the front of his sweatshirt, then jerks back, spilling more.

He and Jessica look at each other.

Jessica clears her throat. She does not wake up bright and sunny like Sam. Her eyes and voice are only half there. It is something I like about her. You should not act all cheery when you have to get up and it is still dark outside, for God's sake. Sam, this means you.

She clears her throat again. "It might snow."

"It is too cold to snow," I inform her. I refrain from saying "you moron," even though, living in Pennsylvania, she should know that.

"I love snow," says Sam, wiping the coffee off his chest with a wet napkin, leaving a trail of shredded paper like snowflakes. Maybe he should not drink coffee. Are Quakers allowed to drink coffee?

I shake my head. He must have Quaker Oats for brains.

"Don't you like snow?" he asks me. His blue eyes twinkle and his curly blond hair looks even bouncier than normal. A grown man should not have bouncy blond hair. Or eyes that twinkle like a two-year-old's. Or be in love with snow.

"Snow sucks," I say, as coldly as I can muster.

Jessica coughs. "Mattie, I need to ask you to watch your language, especially with Rory in the house." She looks down at the Blob sitting on the floor.

"In case you had not noticed," I inform Jessica, "he does not speak."

"He will," she shoots back.

I raise my eyebrows and say "you moron" with my eyes.

Sam and Jessica look at each other again. They do this a lot. I believe it is Quaker-speak. Or they are aliens.

What makes them Quakers, anyway? They do not quake. Except Sam's belly when he laughs. They do not speak Religion like Loopy. In fact, they do not seem to speak Religion at all. Still, I am not exactly overjoyed at this current hostile takeover situation.

The Blob starts banging a blue pot on the floor. He is a drooling land mine planted on the mold and mustard linoleum to torture me. He reaches for me with his grubby hands. I step away. Jessica gives him a sticky roll of kiwi-watermelon-simulation fruit product so his fingers, face, and the floor can get covered with more gack. What is she thinking?

"He's communicating," she says.

I look at her. I want to say, "With what alien life-form?" but her eyes are red and droopy, and she is holding her head at a funny angle.

I guess I am staring at her because she says, "I have a migraine."

"News flash," I say. "Banging pots do not help migraines."

As if he hears me, the Blob stops for a second and utters the sound "duh." Duh is right! Even the Blob can figure it out.

Sam sits his overly large self down on the floor next to the Blob. The floor shakes. Four-point-nine on the Richter scale.

Sam grins at the Blob. "You're starting to talk already, aren't you, bud? Ror-y. That's you. Ror-y."

The Blob lets out a grunt.

Sam claps like he is a kid at the circus. "That's right! Rory!"

The Blob is five years old but looks like two and acts even younger. He has some kind of "severe developmental condition," according to Sam and Jessica. I believe he is a lost cause but they think they can reach him. I do my best to stay out of his reach. But his eyes follow me like a helpless fawn's, trapped in an awkward body. I try to never let his eyes catch me because I do not like helpless and trapped. It makes my stomach queasy.

The Blob catches my eye and I clutch my stomach with one hand, grab my backpack with the other, and head for the front door.

"Don't you want breakfast?" Jessica calls out after me.

"No, thanks."

"Mattie—" Sam starts.

"And do not call me Mattie." I turn to give them my Stay Away stare. "My name is Matt."

I let the storm door slam behind me. I do not like people calling me Mattie. It is Matt. Just Matt. I like it because it sounds like a guy's name and that always throws people off. They do not know what to say, which is good, because I do not wish to talk with them, anyway.

And, of course, Matilda is not an option. That is like a freak-show name. Or so I have been told on numerous occasions. I believe my father named me that as a cruel joke. He was into jokes. And cruelty. Most of the time I hid under the bed.

Oh, good. The bus. Right where Loopy said it would be. I get on and receive a few choice stares. I walk past one girl who says hi. She should save her breath. Nothing personal, but I am not into relationships. You would think that the Black Widow spider painted on my face with mascara would give you a clue. Or my hard stare. Or my outrageous outfit in varying shades of black. I bet you did not know that you can wear pants and a skirt at the same time. With oversized boots from the Goodwill store.

"Weirdo," I hear someone say. I have been called worse.

That is all the attention I get because of what is happening in the back of the bus. I recognize the sneer. The ruthless mocking. The callous laughter. The aching silence of the Victim. It is not me. This time.

I join the lot of the squirming potential Victims as I strain to look away and put myself in another place altogether. It is the universal language of violence. The bully. I shudder and make note of where he is, hoping he sits there all the time. So I can sit far away. *Please.* Stay away.

CHAPTER THREE

am wedged into my guidance counselor's office. It has the size and ambiance of a janitor's closet. And a worse stench. You can get a nicotine fix from the cigarette odor.

The large, bearded guidance counselor is clicking away on his computer. "You took some, uh, tests before you left your last school, and we need to look at those before we place you."

I do not know why only Loopy will call them IQ tests. Perhaps everyone else wants to hide what they really are in case I fail them.

His fingers stop, his eyes open wide, staring at the screen. He whistles.

Oh, God, I failed them.

His eyes dart over to me then back to the screen. He coughs. He puts a hand over his mouth. He looks at me again and then quickly away.

"Am I going to be sent back to middle school?" I ask, unable to bear the silence any longer.

He laughs loudly and awkwardly. "And you're a joker, too, huh?"

Elementary school?

"I think it's safe to say that you're eligible for the accelerated program we have here at Franklin."

Excuse me? Is he saying I am actually smart?

He looks at me over his glasses. "You've been skating by, haven't you? Well, you might actually have to do a little work for a change." He looks back at the screen. "You have to take World Civ with the other ninth-graders because that's a required course to graduate . . . and, hmmm." He raises his eyebrows so high I think his eyeballs might rise above his glasses. "Playing around in math class, were we? Pre-Algebra twice?"

Well, Mr. Jefferson was calm and predictable. And he left me alone. Why would I want to leave that? So I wrote the wrong answers on tests. But really, I like solving equations. Math problems always have a right answer. Unlike my own.

"We'll put you in regular Algebra, but if it's too easy, we can move you up to the accelerated class. All your other classes can be Honors or AP."

"AP?" I whisper. Can I be inconspicuous and AP at the same time?

"A . . . P," he repeats slowly. "You know, advanced placement?"

I nod jerkily.

He types away at the keyboard. "Okay, got to take PE twice a week . . . AP English, AP Biology, and . . . let's see . . . we can't fit Spanish in your schedule, but we'll put you in Honors French."

The implications of being AP are just dawning on my newly enlightened brain. "Does this mean I can graduate early?"

"Yes." He glares at me over his glasses. "But you don't need to rush it."

But if I rush it, I could be done by, say, sixteen and get a job. Or go to college. Or move to Canada. I read on the Internet that you can be declared an adult in Alberta at age sixteen. I could be on my own officially, instead of by default.

"How fast can I graduate?"

He sighs. "You kids, you have no idea how lucky you have it. Like I tell my own kids, you'll realize how tough it is when you're out in the world and don't have Mom and Dad around anymore."

I stare at him like he is the blind man and I am the seeing-eye dog.

"You're only fourteen, right?"

In people years, maybe. In dog years I am ninety-eight. I have lived an entire lifetime.

He shakes his head and hands me my schedule. "One day at a time. It's Friday, so World Civ is your first class. He's expecting you, and he's got a . . . a short fuse. Don't irritate him." He reaches over his desk to open the door. "Go on, now. Hurry. Oh—enjoy your first day."

Enjoy? I am not sure which is worse, first days or nightmares. Actually, first days are nightmares. I have been through enough of them to know that. And this time I get to start with the teacher who has a "short fuse." Exactly the type I try to avoid.

I run all over the stupid school looking for the right room. The building is huge. And not well marked. Since when did C come before A in the alphabet? And what are purple lockers doing in the "Blue Quad"? And why is the "quad" actually a triangle?

When I finally find 3B01, I peek through the window in the door first. The World Civ teacher is balding even though he is not that old. He is talking but he keeps stopping to squeeze his lips together like he is trying to keep his head from exploding. His face is red and I wonder if it always looks that way or if his short fuse is already on fire. I think about not going in at all and, instead, arriving at my second class early. But then I notice that his lips have stopped moving altogether and he is staring straight at me. Through the small window in the door. Which is focusing his beam on me with increasing intensity. His face looks even redder. I want to run but I know that I am trapped.

Slowly I open the door, my heart pounding.

It is still and hot and smells faintly of rotten garbage. All eyes are on me, not just the teacher's. I cannot stand the spotlight but it is shining on me so hard it makes me sweat. Desperately, I lunge for the desk in the back row, out of the teacher's eyeball range. It is just a few steps away but I manage to bang into every other desk and flop into the chair, tipping it noisily.

There are snickers all around me and I hold my breath, hoping the class will just go on. A horrible silence follows. Then the teacher's nasal voice. I swallow so hard my ears are momentarily blocked and I panic, not knowing if he is talking to me, about me, or what.

". . . was saying, I'd like a report on the local, uh, political debate over our role in the Middle East." He clears his throat and I finally breathe.

Until I hear the sneer from a few desks forward and one row to the left and I shiver. I recognize the cruelty in that voice. The bully. From the bus. Why does he have to be in my class?

And then he speaks. "You mean, like, between the real Americans and the pro-terrorist scum?" He snorts.

I look up, surprised that even a bully would talk that way to a teacher.

Amazingly, the teacher is smiling. "I suppose that's one way to put it." He squeezes his lips together again.

I hear a murmur somewhere near me. A murmur of discontent, I am sure.

The bully's black shirt stiffens, his back arches, and he sits up straight. His dark hair is rigid and sticks out at the back of his neck. He raises his head and his nose twitches, sniffing the air, smelling his prey. His head whips around and his small Rat eyes catch me.

I look down fast. Please, let him not have seen me! I was not even the one murmuring, for God's sake. I shift in my seat, leaning on my right hip, to hide behind the boy in front of me.

"Yeah," he says slowly, "I'd put it that way. We've got soldiers fighting to stop the terrorists and keep America safe. Then we got these assholes who won't fight—won't even support our troops—because they're just chicken-shits." He pounds his desk and I jump. "They're trying to stop the war and *help* the terrorists." He snorts, an angry snort. "And they call it *peace*."

He spits the word out but lets the ending hiss linger. It makes me shudder. I remember what Loopy said: *You know how Quakers are into peace.*

I can hear the Rat breathing. I wish he would turn around. Is he still looking at me?

"Yes," the teacher sharply agrees. "People have different ideas about peace, don't they? So, who would like to report on what's happening in our town? Actually, in a lot of towns across the country." He stops to squeeze his mouth shut momentarily. "How do some of the rest of you feel?"

I feel nothing. I just want this class to be over. Someone, please, volunteer to do this report so he does not think to call on the new girl.

For some reason, I look over at the Rat. He is hunkered down and grinning at a student next to him in my row. The Rat squeezes his lips together to the point that his entire face scrunches up in a horrible sneer and turns red. There are muffled snorts of laughter. Is he making fun of the teacher? I wonder if the teacher saw. I glance at the front of the room but the teacher is not looking.

Oh, God, what did the teacher say? Did he just say *Quakers*? I think he did. *Any Quakers?* Why would he say that? And why is he looking at me? Does he know? How could he know? I am not a Quaker, I just live with them. It was not my choice!

"How about our new student, Misssss . . ."

Oh, God! He knows! I refuse to look up.

"Hmm?" he insists.

The only sound is the static hum from the fluorescent lights. Their *buzz—crack!* makes my ears throb. My eyes are blinking as frenetically as the lights flicker. My arms and legs are starting to shake. That familiar, awful feeling. I wind my legs around each other, grip the edge of the desk, and stare at the gouged-out blob in the middle of it.

At the front of the room, papers rustle and finally snap. "Matil—"

"No," I squeak-scream before the teacher even has my name out.

"Excuse me?" His voice goes up. "No?"

I shake my head, still looking down at the gouge on my desk. "I—I—" I cannot even think, much less speak. "Not—I—I—am—um—not—"

The Rat snorts. "Uh—I—ah—ew—ahn—*DUH!*" I can feel him turn in his desk but I crouch down, out of his radar, I hope.

Snickering, and then the teacher's voice again.

I hold my breath.

"No takers, then?" he says.

Takers? Oh, God, *that's* what he was saying. Not *Quakers!* *Takers.* I let out my breath and almost allow my head to drop the last few inches to the desk.

I hate first days.

"Hey, I care about this stuff," the Rat says. "I'll do an oral report, but I don't want to write one. And can you make it count as my grade if, you know, I don't ace the final?"

What? Involuntarily, I glance at the teacher. Is he going to let the Rat get away with that? Again, I am surprised at his response. His eyes are soft and he nods his head and looks at the Rat the way a father might look at his son, whom everyone else knows is obnoxious, but the father is too blind to see.

"I guess," the Rat says, turning around to look in my direction, "some people don't give a damn about our troops getting killed over there, trying to save our lives."

I care! I hate anyone even getting hurt, much less dying!

I hate to see anyone being a victim! How dare he make me look like someone who does not even care? Does he really care about dying soldiers? I wonder. He seems to care more about creating turmoil.

I look back at the teacher and his soft eyes have turned to fire and they are burning into me. This is not a good beginning.

BAAAAAAAAAAAAAAH! The electronic bell over the door makes me jump. Scuffling, and boots, and chatter move past me and I get up slowly, stiffly, and stagger out into the hall.

The hair on the back of my neck stands up even before the hot breath hits me. The hiss is low but the tension is high. "Chicken-shit."

I whip around to see the narrowed eyes and ugly sneer of the Rat. He laughs mockingly and elbows a boy next to him, who starts laughing, too. The Rat stands shoulder to shoulder with several more of his Vermin. They blend into one massive Wall as they block the hallway, leering at me. I turn and run the other way.

I shake through my entire English class until the blaring bell jangles me again.

By the time I get to math, I am calmer. It is almost Zen to sit and do math problems. Algebra is the antithesis of World Civ. The teacher is boring, predictable, and relatively safe. He has about as much personality as a school bus driver. He sits at his desk and ignores us while we copy problems off the board and write the answers in our notebooks. At least, some of us do. Even those who refuse to work leave me alone. They throw spitballs, play games on PDAs, and trade medications. It is much like being on the bus. But without the Rat. I suspect the Rat is only in World Civ, although in his case "only" is still too much.

I have no appetite for lunch but I am on the lunch program and at my last school the Cafeteria Police called Loopy if I did not pick up the lovely rations. So I get my tray and slump at a table with some large, loud girls who smell bad, figuring I am safe because no one will mess with them, not even the Rat. They give me strange looks but shrug and go on with their raunchy jokes. I pick at the barf on my Styrofoam plate, trying to decide if it is Lasagna à la Piemonte or Mediterranean Trout Treasure. I do not eat any of it. I drink a soda, and that fills me up without making me sick.

I am in French 5, which is a little odd, considering I have only had two years of French. Still, my last French teacher told me that I have a *"bi-zarre"* facility for languages. I thought it was an idiot-savant sort of thing, like I am particularly good at languages but I am otherwise particularly stupid. Except that, apparently, I am not otherwise particularly stupid. Now that is truly *bi-zarre.*

We are studying French literature. Madame insists that we speak *"en français, s'il vous plaît."* This does not actually bother me because it is like speaking in code. I imagine myself in the French resistance and everything I say to the co-opted Vichy French teacher is a lie, a façade to obtain an A but never tell her what I really think of Albert Camus . . . *merde!*

Biology is good. I am an expert. We are studying morphing, but I have already morphed. I have my own exoskeleton. My face is hard and cold like stone. My shoulders are piles of knots strung together into steel. My muscles are so hard they are like bone.

I have spent years developing my armor and I will not let it be pierced.

On the bus, I sit near the front, away from where the Rat hole is, I hope. Rats carry plague and must be avoided. I learned that a long time ago. I stay low, digging in my backpack for some imaginary need, wanting to slump so far down that I can hide under the seat. I make myself small and dark so that I look like a hole and there is nothing there. *Nothing, Rat, only nothingness, so move on.* I sense him slink past and I am safe for the moment. I know, however, that it is only a matter of time before I am dead meat.

CHAPTER FOUR

The first day of school seems like a week and I spend Saturday in my room recuperating. It is actually Jessica and Sam's room, I suppose, since this house has only two bedrooms and the Blob has the tiny one next to mine. Jessica and Sam sleep in the living room downstairs.

There is not much in my room except the sofa bed, dresser, and shelves filled with an odd assortment of books— *Contact, A Beautiful Mind, Fine Woodworking*—and a cross-stitch on the wall that says "Be the change you want to see in the world.—*Mahatma Gandhi*." I was not aware that Gandhi was a Quaker. I imagine it would be news to him, too.

By Sunday, I am ready to see the Quaker Trio in the "family" room, aka kitchen.

Jessica fixes a big breakfast.

Scrapple: I call it the *s* word with *crap* inside of it.

Eggs: aborted animals.

Burnt toast: dead bread.

No apple crisp.

I eat nothing.

"It's First Day," Jessica says.

I think this is some special occasion. "First day of what?"

"I mean it's Sunday, the first day of the week. We have Meeting for Worship this morning."

"You mean church?" I try to put it in normal words for her.

"Well, it's our version of church."

"Oh, no thanks. Been there, done that." I have been to so many churches—fundamentalist, revivalist, and even regular ones—it is ridiculous. And so are they.

"There's no child care at Meeting this week," Jessica pipes up. "I was going to stay home with Rory so you could go, but if you don't mind staying home and taking care of him—"

"Whoa! Okay, I understand blackmail. I will go." No way am I being stuck with the Blob.

I am out the door while they are still staring at each other in Quaker. I crunch over the frozen grass to their Subaru station wagon. It is white. And rust. With a lime-green passenger door. And a peace symbol on the back. And a bumper sticker that says I SUPPORT OUR TROOPS, I QUESTION OUR POLICIES. The bumper is crushed right next to the sticker, and I wonder if an angry vehicle was responding to the statement.

Sam catches up with me. I stop breathing when I see his dorky hat. It is a too-small baseball cap that makes his hair stick out in curly clumps on the sides. He looks like a clown.

He is wheezing. The man needs to go on a diet. And get some exercise. He will be dead by the time he is forty. Oh, God, I sound like a public service announcement.

"You don't have to go to Meeting if you don't want to." He pants. "You're welcome, but you're not compelled."

Another breath. "Jessica will stay home with you and Rory, if you like."

I ponder my stellar options. I look back at the dumpy duplex, then at the sucky Subaru. I am freezing. The Subaru is closer. "Fine, I will go to your Meeting."

"We don't proselytize," he says. Big word for a clown. "Quakers don't try to convert people."

"I said I would go." A shiver runs through me. "See, I just quaked."

"You really don't have to—"

"Could you unlock the car? Please?" I am stuck in *Little Subaru on the Prairie* and Pa won't open the door.

Finally, I am sitting in the front seat, arms folded, shivering. I look down at the shredded seats. "Which one of you had the tantrum with the knife?"

Sam chuckles. "This is one of those 'previously owned vehicles.' I don't know anything about the seats. Or the dents in the doors." He shrugs his Michelin Man shoulders, almost like he is embarrassed.

"It is all right. I understand 'used,'" I say grimly.

He smiles. The clown misses the irony.

He shoves a hand in his pocket and pulls out an open roll of wintergreen LifeSavers with the wrapper dangling. "Would you like a mint?"

"Why? Does my breath stink?" My arms are still folded.

He laughs. "No. Come on, have one."

I reach out, rip more of the wrapper off, and take one, cautiously. Quickly, before he has the chance to make a snide remark, I say, "It will not make me sweet."

"Aw, you're already sweet," he says, stuffing the candy back in his pocket.

"You are mistaken," I say. And you are not very bright.

"You're a little prickly on the outside, maybe, but I don't blame you. I know you're a sweet kid inside, though."

"What makes you so delusional?"

He shrugs. "An old Quaker idea."

"Excuse me?"

"There's something of God in everyone."

I stare at him. "Perhaps I inherited His bad side."

He just smiles, crunching his candy.

It is an annoying sound.

"You will break your teeth," I warn him.

"The great thing about wintergreen LifeSavers is that they spark."

I do not follow his logic. Then I realize he has none. "What?"

"Haven't you tried that before? Here, you've got to take the rest of the roll." He struggles to get the candy out of the pocket of his green down vest again and the car jerks around the road.

I roll my eyes.

"No, really," he says. "Take these and go stand in a totally dark room and look in a mirror—"

"I will not be able to see anything in a totally dark room," I point out.

"But you will! If you bite through wintergreen LifeSavers—with your mouth open—you'll see sparks!"

I stare at him. He is a child in a grown-up body. Peter Pan swallowed up by the Incredible Hulk. And the Hulk is shoving LifeSavers into my hand.

I take them and look at them. Something stirs deep inside my head. It is my mother. I remember—I think I remember—her giving me LifeSavers. Like this. Partially opened. And they were mint. Maybe spearmint. I do not know. But they were white. They looked like this. Just like this. I cannot stop staring at the LifeSavers in my hand.

"Hey!" Sam cries, making me jump. He points past me, out of my side window. "Look at the way the mist just hangs over the river like that!"

It does not take much to amuse Sam, apparently.

"Nice," I say dully.

He is not put off. "Isn't it incredible?"

I sigh. "Actually, it is called science."

He looks at me.

"Wa-ter va-por," I say slowly, on the off chance that he might understand.

He grins like an imp, if imps are crazy, annoying creatures. And he imitates my speech pattern. "I—think—it's—God."

"God as water vapor. Nice, Sam. I am not sure He—or She—would go along with it, though."

He grins. "Why not? God is all around us."

Oh, really? I sincerely doubt that, Sam. He was never around at 125 South Water Street, apartment 416. He never stopped the rock-hard hand from finding my mother. Or me. No matter where I hid. No matter how fast I ran. No matter how many times I begged him to stop. Where was God then? No one ever has a good answer for that. They look away. Or down. Or worse, they look at you with pain oozing from their eyes and you do not know whether the pain is theirs or yours. And whether you have brought more pain into the world by opening your big mouth. And whether all the pain was your fault to begin with.

Sam is staring at me. What? Was I supposed to answer him? His eyes are not twinkling. He is not chuckling. His belly is not shaking. So, what is that noise? Oh, it is my foot kicking the dashboard. Hard. Over and over. I stop.

"Are you all right?" His voice is soft and marshmallowy.

"Of course. My toe was itching. That is all. It is hard to get at it in these boots. So I have to kick."

He does not say anything but watches the road ahead. I steal a look at him. He is wearing the saddest clown face I have ever seen and I have to look away. The mist from the river is getting in my eyes.

CHAPTER FIVE

I am sitting in a big, blank, cold room staring at a bunch of people. Who are all staring back at me. The chairs are in a circle. It appears that we are going to play Duck, Duck, Goose.

This is the Meeting House. It is not a church, I am informed. It is, in fact, a small, shabby house in the middle of a run-down neighborhood not far from Casa Quaker. We are sitting in what is probably supposed to be the living room. Only without furniture, except for these metal folding chairs. Also, there is no steeple. No cross. No altar. Outside, there is no brightly lit church sign with a thought-provoking query like, *Where will YOU spend eternity—smoking or nonsmoking?* There is only a small sign on the porch railing that states the hours of worship and a banner underneath saying PEACE ON EARTH in red and gold letters. I am thinking they forgot to take down their Christmas decorations.

I pick flakes of black polish off my nails. I look at my watch. I squirm in my cold, hard chair next to Sam's. "When is the service going to begin?" I hiss.

Sam smiles, then grins his impish grin and whispers, "This is worship, Matt."

I glare at him. "No, really. How much longer do we have to wait?"

Some old lady throws me a "be quiet, young lady" look. Sam just smiles.

I am confused.

If this is "worship," then Quakers bring a whole new meaning to the term "religion." They are not born-again. They are born-dead. At least, that is what it looks like when they are in church. I mean, in Meeting. It is not like a meeting of the yearbook committee or Scouts. There is no talking, no music, no singing. No pictures, no reading, no words. Everyone simply sits frozen in this room staring at each other or closing their eyes, napping, apparently. God knows there is nothing to look at except white walls and large windows, which are up high enough that you can see trees and sky but nothing more.

Now I understand why Sam told me it is okay to say something in Meeting if you are moved to speak. It would break the monotony. I am almost moved to say, "Blue-light special! Bible sale at Kmart! Buy one, get one free!" But it is easier to simply ignore the situation. It is a skill I have perfected over the years.

I notice a newspaper on the floor under the chair next to me. It is open to the editorial page. I bend forward and turn my head to read one of the articles because at least it is something to do. Someone has highlighted certain phrases in yellow so I cannot help but read those first. *Do we think we own the world and can make over every country in our own image? We already have the Midwest U.S. Are we looking to create the Mid-East U.S., too?* I appreciate the article's sarcasm. I imagine it would be lost on my World Civ teacher, however. The yellow highlight also leads me to *How many people have to die?* That is the part I hate. The killing. The dying. The pain.

I am at the fold in the newspaper now so I grab it to read the rest. But then I realize how much noise a newspaper makes in a silent room and I look up and see everyone's eyes on me and I quickly let go and sink farther in my chair. I glance over at Sam in case he is angry and I need to scoot my chair away from him. He catches my glance and gives me a smile, so I am safe.

I am still bored, however. In fact, I am so bored I am practically asleep when someone finally stands up. Everyone is shaking hands with each other and chatting as if the Meeting is a big success. Now here is a club I would not mind being the secretary for . . . *Meeting Minutes for Sunday, January 7: Nothing happened. Hallelujah! The end.*

I rush out to the Subaru half a block away to impress upon Sam that we are not staying for "fellowship" or however you say "coffee and doughnuts" in Quaker. After a couple of minutes, he is on the front steps looking toward the Subaru and me. I sigh dramatically, hoping he will notice. He does, but motions me to come back to the Meeting House. I shake my head and stare at the car.

He does not come immediately. I look back and he is talking with a group of people and shaking his head, but not at me. He is pulling at his watch strap like it is cutting off his circulation. The circulation to my toes is cut off because they are so numb. I lean dramatically against the car.

In a moment he is there. "It's not locked," he says.

I get in and stare at him because it was locked before and how was I supposed to know?

He reads my mind and answers, "Jessica always locks it, but I never do. Hey, Matt, we usually stay after Meeting to sing a song. And I wanted to introduce you to some folks."

I fold my arms and look away.

"Well, maybe next time," he says.

If there is a next time.

Sam clears his throat. "I need to make a slight detour on the way home."

Probably to get the doughnuts I have deprived him of. I sigh and continue to stare out my window.

When he pulls the car to a stop and starts plucking at his watch again, I finally look over at him. He is staring out his window. I notice that it is not a watch he keeps fiddling with, but a bracelet. The man is wearing a silver bracelet. It adds nothing to the baseball cap motif.

"That church has been helping war victims in a lot of Mid-East countries," Sam says, out of the blue.

"What?"

He turns to look at me. "That Catholic Church."

As I stare at him and try to make sense of what he is saying, I see past him to a large stone building. When I look closer, I see nasty words painted on the stone in red paint. And a broken window. I lean over to see more and notice the sign out front: OUR LADY OF PEACE.

Peace. That word again. Peace, the thing the Rat decries.

"This vandalism," Sam says, pointing at Our Lady of Peace, "started after the news broke about the ring of terrorist plots on the bridges and tunnels in New York, Washington, and San Francisco."

"But nothing actually happened," I remind him.

"No, but we were brought right back to the terrorist

attacks on September eleventh. That horrible fear. The unpredictability. The feeling of being a target."

I understand that. Very well.

Sam sighs. "Once again, being against the war is seen as unpatriotic. And *peace* has become a dirty word." He shrugs and smiles. "It just means we have to say it even louder."

"Why?" It is out of my mouth before I can stop it.

His blue eyes gaze at me sadly, gently. "Because ... I don't want anyone else to die." He looks almost disappointed before he turns away again.

I understand his point but I do not understand his desire to act. It does not matter if you are right. What matters is self-preservation. Somewhere along the way, Sam, you missed the raison d'être, the whole meaning of life: If you will draw negative attention to yourself, it is better to Shut Up.

All the same, as I read the threats splattered across Our Lady of Peace, I wonder why people choose to be violent when we are all facing violence from the outside.

And I am just the tiniest bit ticked off that Sam would give me a disappointed look simply because I know enough to stay out of the spotlight.

Sam pulls at his bracelet again, making scratching metal sounds. It is so annoying.

"Would you stop doing that?"

He looks at me, his eyes big. "What?"

"Flicking your bracelet."

He looks down at it, almost like he is surprised that it is there, and shoves it quickly under the sleeve of his sweat-shirt. "It—it's nothing." He looks back at me like a kid who is denying stealing cookies even though his mouth is full.

It is too late. I have already seen it. And he is a very bad liar.

When we get back to Casa Quaker, the Blob is moaning and drooling as usual.

Jessica is rubbing her forehead. She stops and asks me how I "enjoyed" Meeting.

"You mean Sit-and-Stare?"

She smiles. "We have unprogrammed Meetings. What we're doing is listening."

"Oh." I make my face look serious and concerned. "Has anyone noticed yet that no one is speaking?"

Sam sits down at the kitchen table with the Blob drooling in his lap. "Sometimes people speak, if they're moved to."

The Blob is moved to bang the plates with a fork. My fork.

I yank the fork out of his hand and sit down at my spot on the other side of Sam, gathering all my dishes as far away as possible from the gack attack.

I wipe the fork off with my blue paper napkin that does not go with the kitchen's mustard and mold motif. Jessica does not seem to notice such things. "So you are just waiting to see if someone might speak? You have a very high tolerance for disappointment."

Jessica ladles lima beans onto our plates out of a blue dented pot. I know it has been washed since the Blob played with it because she treats it like another baby. It is her favorite pot. It is very special. It belonged to her grandmother, you know.

"We're also waiting for God," Jessica says.

I knew God-speak would have to crop up at some point.

I drop my fork on the table in mock shock. "The Second Coming?"

Sam chuckles. I should start calling him Chuckles the Clown. "No. We're listening for . . . a voice."

"Oh," I say. Again, I put on my thoughtful look. "It might help if you hired a minister."

Jessica opens her mouth but Sam holds up his hand. "Just sit and listen, if you like. You might hear something helpful."

"First, I will need to learn Quaker-speak," I point out. "You people communicate telepathically. I believe you are an alien race."

They laugh as if I am joking.

While Jessica spoons out the mashed potatoes and meat loaf, Sam tells her that I asked him when the service would begin. He winks at her. Then they both say together, "The service begins when the worship ends." And they laugh again. They are easily amused.

Sam turns to me. "You see, service is helping others. And that's what we do *after* Meeting." He is still grinning. "Get it?"

I stare at him. "If that is Quaker humor, you people should stick to oatmeal."

After lunch, I try to escape upstairs to read but Jessica stops me. "I could use some help with the dishes."

I look over at the dishwasher to give her a hint. That is what it is for. She does not get it and tells me to bring the plates over from the table. I want to say "Why? Have you suddenly suffered some debilitating injury?" but I do not. I think of what Loopy said: *This is the end of the line for you.* I need to stay here long enough to graduate and get to Canada.

So, I sigh and slowly retrieve dishes, one by one, from the table and place them randomly in the dishwasher. I also pick up the blue confetti I have made out of my napkin and put it in the trash. I am a napkin shredder. I always have been. Loopy says it is a nervous habit. I believe it is a sign that blue does not go with the mid-twentieth century mustard and mold décor.

"I see you didn't eat much meat loaf," Jessica comments. She is almost right. I did not eat any meat loaf. "Are you a vegetarian?"

"That depends. I am a vegetarian when it comes to meat loaf and turkey. Hot dogs and chicken nuggets are all right because they can hardly be accused of containing any actual meat."

"I see." She nods as if what I am saying is serious. "How do you feel about the food at the school cafeteria?"

"You mean, the barfeteria?"

She smiles. "I'm worried about how thin you are, Matt. You hardly eat any breakfast, and I'm afraid you're not eating at school, either."

"Going through the barfeteria line is comparable to pass-ing through an entire row of ripe Porta Pottis."

She screws up her face. "Would you like me to pack your lunch?"

I am not sure what to say.

"I'll make a lunch for you every day, as long as you tell me what you like to eat."

I shrug. "Okay."

"So, what do you like?"

"Junk food."

She laughs. "I'd like to fix you some healthy things, like spinach balls."

"You are joking, right?"

"No, they're really very good. I'll make some. If you like them, I'll pack some in your lunch."

I decide I need to put her on the right track. "How about apples?"

"Sure."

"Grapes?"

"Okay."

"I despise bananas."

"No bananas. How about cheese? You love cheese."

How does she know I love cheese? Oh, right, I have been eating here for almost a week, so she is noticing my eating habits. I am not sure I like that. "I hate cheese."

She raises her eyebrows but drops them quickly. "Okay."

We have plain macaroni for dinner. No cheese. Sam complains. Jessica pats his hand and informs him that he needs to cut down on fat. He cannot argue with her. But he looks like a puppy whose owner is taking his favorite slipper away from him. I understand. My mouth is watering for cheese.

After dinner, I am craving cheese so badly I am drooling. Sam and Jessica are upstairs giving the Blob a bath. Apparently, it is a two-person job. I find some cheese in the fridge drawer. Sharp cheddar. I break off a piece and cram it in my mouth.

Jessica walks in.

I freeze and stick the wad of cheese under my tongue. "What?" I say it in an accusing fashion to put her off. A good offense is the best defense. That is the only useful information to be gleaned from organized sports.

"Nothing." But she looks suspicious. When she turns her head, I chew fast. She walks over to the sink and starts washing apples, talking to me over her shoulder. "How was school? Do you feel like you'll fit in okay?"

I quickly swallow the cheese. "I do not 'fit in,' Jessica. I simply go unnoticed. That is part of who I am. I am not going to change."

She turns the running water off, dries her hands, and speaks softly. "I'm not trying to change you."

I do not believe her. "I am not changing the way I dress, either. I am a fashion plate."

"I like the way you dress."

I stare at her. "You are odd, Jessica, truly odd. Has anyone ever informed you of that?"

She laughs as she pumps hand cream out of the pink bottle by the sink. I can smell the raspberry scent from here. "Many times."

Great, I have been sent to live with the odd ones out. "So, are you and your . . . Meeting . . . about the only Quakers left in the world, or what?"

She laughs. She is too happy. Or perhaps she is on drugs. "We may not be a large group, but there are some of us all over the world. A lot in Kenya."

I stare at her. I guess I should be grateful that they live here and Loopy did not have to send me to Africa. Or maybe Africa would not be so bad. If I could not speak the language, then no one would expect me to talk. I could still think all my snide remarks in my head. It would be like a continuous criticism of a silent movie.

But it is not silent in the Quaker kitchen anymore. Sam is back, carrying the Blob in a rare, clean moment. The Blob is moaning and reaching for the pot on the stove.

"I need to do my homework," I lie. I can easily do it during class and on the bus. But it is a good excuse to get away.

"You know," says Jessica, tilting her head and walking toward me, "the only thing you might want to try is pulling your hair back a little so we could all see you better. You have such beautiful skin and haunting eyes. You're a very attractive girl, Matt."

I look away as she talks, like when someone is lecturing me.

She smiles and strokes my hair as I turn to go upstairs. I pull away and take the steps two at a time. It is tingly and raspberryish where she touched my hair. At the top of the stairs, I stop before going into my room. I take a few steps down the hall and turn the bathroom light on. I peek in at the mirror briefly. Just out of curiosity, not because I care. And I am right. There is no very attractive girl in there. The girl in the mirror has a nose too big for her pinched-up face. She has dark, shifty eyes. She is a hideous tetrahedron frizz head. And she must remain unnoticed.

I slap the light switch off.

Quakers are blind, apparently.

CHAPTER SIX

I hate World Civilization. Not the concept. My class. And the Rat. And the teacher, whose name, I discover, is Mr. Morehead. It is not a good name for a high school teacher. For many reasons. Use your imagination. I save him from his unfortunate fate by renaming him Mr. Warhead because that is what he is. Truly. He is obsessed with war, fighting, and the way I see it, beating the crap out of every non-American. He calls it Bringing Freedom and Democracy to the World. My advice to anyone who hears those words in any country other than This Great Nation of Ours is "Run away!"

Today he is fixating on the prime minister of Great Britain, whom he thinks is a "little snot." I do not know the man personally, so I can neither confirm nor deny that assessment. However, when Mr. Warhead says "snot" for the million and tenth time, I cannot help but look at his nose. My stomach curls into a million and ten knots. The man has large hairs growing out of his nostrils, like someone shoved a bonsai tree up there and the roots are still dangling, looking for a place to plant themselves.

I must have a look of sick horror on my face because Mr. Warhead sees me and squeezes his mouth shut in that odd way he has. "Yes, frightening, isn't it?" he says in his nasal voice. "But, make no mistake, our troops are the best in the world and our flag will rise above it all."

I am picturing an American flag rising over his nose hairs.

It is not a patriotic sight.

I return to my position of anonymity in the back of the classroom. There is some safety in numbers and it is a large class. Unfortunately, Mr. Warhead believes in old-fashioned rows so he can walk up and down in between them when the mood strikes. I cannot stand that, especially when he turns and walks up behind me. I am waiting for him to smack the back of my head, even though I know teachers are not allowed to do this. It is hard for me to shake old habits. And what is to stop him, really?

I do not want to see his red face or hirsute nostrils, so I concentrate on my desk. It is the usual fake plastic-wood kind, with a triangular gouge exposing the darker layer underneath. People have filled in the mark with varying shades of blue and black, like an oozing bruise. I do the same when I am not writing down Mr. Warhead's rants.

He spends twenty minutes telling us why the United States does not need to give in to "liberal" United Nations resolutions or even the Geneva Convention. After which he announces, "Pop quiz!"

The class groans. Binders snap, papers rustle, and pens clack as everyone gets ready for the quiz. I wonder what it will be today. On Monday, it was "Middle Eastern Theater" geography. I was one of the few not to fail the quiz, although Mr. Warhead drew a big red question mark over my heading: "The Mid-East . . . U.S."

"Dude!" It is the Rat. "Don't you want me to give my report?"

It is so obviously a stall tactic.

But Mr. Warhead turns around from the board and his face is all soft and mushy. "I'm sorry, Richard. Go ahead, but please try to be quick."

The Rat takes a deep breath, slowly, and cracks his knuckles. "Well, like, we're fighting terrorists, right? The United States, I mean, with hardly anyone else helping us. Because the rest of them are all chicken-shits. So we're out there doing it for everyone. And what do we get? People ragging on us. I mean, it's like they've all taken some drug and they've lost their brains."

Mr. Warhead is nodding but holds up his hand. "And, specifically, what have reactions been in our own town?"

"Oh, yeah, well, we got these—what do you call those businesses that don't even know how to make money?"

Mr. Warhead smirks. "Nonprofits?"

"Yeah, these nonprofits that decide we should stop fighting the terrorists." He grins slowly. "So, their offices get bombed with pigs' blood. Kind of a wake-up call. The police"—and his grin turns into a leer—"aren't too upset, you know? Because, hey, the people who did the deed are, like, patriots."

"Patriots?" someone mutters.

The Rat whips around, not to me, fortunately. "Yeah, patriots! Ever heard of the Boston Tea Party? When our rights and freedoms are being taken away, we have to fight back."

Against a nonprofit?

The Rat turns back around. "Then the mosque gets hit because, well," and he shrugs.

Oh, I see, because they are Muslim and, by definition, are all terrorists? God! I may not believe in religion but I do believe in leaving people alone if they are not bothering anyone. I cannot believe the crap coming out of the Rat's mouth.

"All the public opinion polls prove," the Rat says, "that Americans pretty much support the president and support the war because, like"—he looks around the room—"we're Americans, right? The rest of them are chicken-shits!"

I want to shout "Fact or opinion!" like Miss Barnes, my World Civ teacher at my old school. She did that all the time whenever we gave a report or even answered a question. It was so annoying. Now I wish she were here.

His Vermin applaud loudly. A red-faced Mr. Warhead nods, seriously, his lips tightly shut, like he is believing all of it.

"I mean, what's with them?" the Rat continues. "Do they want the terrorists to take over? Don't they care about freedom and democracy? I'm going to fight for this country and our way of life, whatever it takes." He pounds his desk for effect. He is almost grinning he is so amused by his performance.

He has pounded Mr. Warhead into a frenzy. The man's face is now a purplish shade of red and his lips are squished together so tightly I think his head might burst. His mouth barely opens as he squeezes out, "Nice job, Richard."

He turns and writes on the board, hard, like he is trying to hammer through it. The marker squeaks and cries plaintively under his heavy hand. *Name the senators supporting the war effort.*

He whips back around, looking at his watch. "You have five minutes!"

"Aw, man." The Rat rolls his eyes and the grin is gone.

"Good try, dude," the guy next to him whispers.

"Yeah, whatever," the Rat replies.

Whatever? *Whatever?* How can he say that? He is such a Rat! A scavenger! Feeding on the emotions of other people. Like this warped teacher's, who obviously has some serious problem.

I make a heading on my page and scribble down the names of Mr. Warhead's favorite senators while some people scratch their heads and others look earnestly out of the window at the snow. I look at them like they are idiots. How can they not know? Mr. Warhead talks about the Good Pro-War Senators constantly, as if they are all close friends of his. He quotes their brilliant sound bites like my favorite, "You're either with us or with them." Apparently, there is no room for debate in our democratic society.

We pass our papers to the front and it is almost time for the bell, finally.

Mr. Warhead reminds us of the pages to read in our textbook and how we will need our class notes to be able to answer all of the questions at the end of chapter three and do we all understand, *"Matilda?"*

I shudder, dropping my pen. The Rat snickers. I look up at Mr. Warhead and give him a jerky nod. Mr. Warhead insists upon calling me Matilda, which makes the Rat laugh, and I hate him for that. He does it on purpose. It puts a spotlight on me whenever he says my name, reminding the Rat that I am a potential Victim, and Mr. Warhead knows it. Just because the Rat marked me as someone who does not care. I have to scurry off to my next class before the Rat can catch me, hide on the bus so the Rat does not even realize I am there, and avoid my locker because, by some hideous twist of fate, our lockers are practically next to each other.

I suffer through World Civ four times a week, at different time slots, depending on the day. I imagine it is somewhat like experiencing random terrorist bombings throughout an otherwise frightening but mostly uneventful week.

In English, on the other hand, I am all-powerful. Mrs. Jimenez must have seen my IQ test results. She treats me as if I am the Mighty Queen of World Literature. She cowers as she walks by my desk, so much so that she has to look up at me even though I am sitting. It is as if she is frightened to speak in front of me, in case she makes a mistake and I am forced to yell, "Off with her head!"

She gives me As on anything I write. I believe she would give me an A for writing my name. Even if I misspelled it. She does not tell me what she really thinks. She simply writes meaningless words like *outstanding, superb, amazing* in the margin. She is not grading my writing. She is grading my IQ.

Lunch is the usual horror. I spend it in the girls' bathroom, the one place where I am certain the Rat cannot find me. I open the lunch bag from Jessica. An apple, some grapes, a juice box, and a granola bar. I manage to drink the juice because it is apple but I save the food. It is hard to eat when you are hovering on the edge of nausea.

The bell rings and I groan, remembering where I have to go next.

PE.

Putrid Exercise.

Painful Exhibitionism.

Please Erase.

I cannot compete with the Amazon Women Jockettes. Nor do I want to. After a week of being trampled in volleyball, basketball, and some form of cruel obstacle relay that looks like it came out of *Alice in Wonderland,* I decide to escape. I already know that Miss Splits—I kid you not, and she was a gymnast—checks the bathroom and the bleachers for runaways, but once in a while I can get away with it. I find the perfect hiding place. A locker. It is like being under a bed, only vertical. Somewhat cramped, but it beats the alternative. I simply get out when I hear the girls' voices coming and act as if I am the first one to arrive. One girl looks at me, her eyes narrowing. But then her Cool Blond Friend asks her if she brought that Cool Blond shampoo and I am off the radar screen again. Life returns to normal for the time being.

Until 3:40 P.M., to be precise.

I am opening my locker, taking my World Civ notes out. For some stupid reason, I look up. And see him.

The Rat.

He is strutting his camo legs over to me, leering at me, sneering, his nose twitching like he smells fresh kill.

The quaking begins. I look down at my notes. World Civilization is trembling in my hands. *Do not make eye contact!* I look away. *Hide!* I drop to my knees, shaking. I scrounge. Around the bottom of my locker. To hide my arms. Which are flailing, jumping. *Pray!* In case there is a God.

I see a tattooed arm. It grabs the lock on his locker. I flinch. Waiting for his other arm to attack. *Tuck your neck in!* I crouch. *Brace your shoulders!* I do. But they are still jumping. Like an electrified frog. Even after it is decapitated.

The Rat does a war whoop. I am sure it is The End.

"Hey!" his oily voice booms in my ear.

I jump. I see his greasy black hair. *Close your eyes! Do not look into the blackness!* I hold my breath. My head will burst. My body will explode.

I hear the crash and jangle of metal. A body slammed against a locker.

It is not mine.

But I still jump.

I hear a groan.

It is also not mine.

But it makes my eyes water just to hear it.

The Rat laughs. He hisses something I cannot make out.

"I—I don't know, man!" a strangled voice yelps.

And everyone else laughs, the nervous laughter of the terrified, teetering on the edge of being Victims themselves.

My body shivers and quakes even more, and the nausea rises from my stomach to my throat like a mushroom cloud. I clench my mouth shut. I hold my arms down for fear they will start flailing wildly, uncontrollably, and the Rat will notice me. I hope he cannot see my twitching legs, my shaking body, or his beady eyes will catch me and I will be Rat meat.

I want to tell him to stop, to stop hurting the Victim, but mostly I want to run and hide. I wish there were a bed to crawl under. I have been there before. I pretend I am not here. I am hoping that will make the Rat disappear.

The second dismissal bell rings. There is noise and commotion and I do not feel the Rat near me anymore. I refuse to look up, though, just in case. I shut my locker door and run all the way to the bus.

The Rat struts onto the bus, on a violence high from

slamming that boy against the locker. You would think that choking someone would be enough of a thrill for one day and that maybe the Rat will be happy now and back off. But no. Violence is a drug and the Rat is an addict. He will always want more, crave more. I know that. I touch the scar at the nape of my neck. I know.

He kicks my backpack and laughs. I reach out and grab it, pulling it toward me. I do not come up for air. I stare at the muddy brown footprints smeared on the rubber-ribbed floor of the bus. I see a wad of gray gum stuck to the side of the bus. I examine a torn piece of spiral notebook paper under the seat in front of me and count the frills remaining from where it was ripped from the spiral.

The Rat is laughing his hideous laugh. I do not know if he is laughing at me or another Victim. I am shaking again. The tornado rises from inside and spins around until I think there is no way to stop myself from spinning in circles. I wrap my arms around my legs. But that does not stop the shaking. It does make me into a small quivering ball, though, and maybe I am small enough that the Rat will not notice me.

It works for today, but someday my luck will run out.

And I do not know how to handle bullies. I never have.

I should be an expert. However, it is my belief that no one can stop Beasts. Only Beasts can stop themselves. By getting arrested, killed, or because they want to reform. Personally, I only meet the reformed kind in books, so I am forced to deal with the others. Over and over.

I want to put them all on a rocket to Mars. Not a space shuttle. Shuttle implies that they would come back again. And what good would that be? I have been in school for so many years now that I have an entire fleet of rockets booked.

In grade school they tell you just to give the Beasts "I" messages:

I feel hurt when you kick me.

I do not like it when you tease me and make me cry.

I would appreciate it if you would stop shoving your fist into my ribs repeatedly.

By second grade, even the stupidest kids figure out that saying "I feel bad when you hurt me" only encourages the Beasts. The Beasts have their own "I" messages:

I feel great that I am hurting you.

I am happy that you are suffering.

I will continue terrorizing you, now that I know how successful I truly am.

"I" messages do not stop them from saying that you are ugly. Or stupid. Or that they are bigger and stronger than you and they will get you somewhere, sometime, no matter what.

get off the bus and I can breathe again. When I reach the house, Sam is driving up in the Subaru. He gets out, smiling and waving. "Hi, Matt! How was your day?"

I shrug. It is nicer than saying "crappy."

He grabs about a dozen plastic grocery bags at once from the backseat of the car, closing the door with his foot.

I decide I can hold the storm door open for him. The top of the door snags the hem of the PACE flag.

He looks up at it. "It's starting to sag. Guess I need to fix that."

"What is the deal with this, anyway?" I know now that their last name is Fox.

He stops and stares at me. "You've never seen one of these? It's a peace flag. *Pah-chay.* That's Italian for peace."

Oh. Italian is not one of my languages. And I am not sure that marking your house with a flag that screams "peace" is such a good idea these days.

I sigh and follow Sam inside.

"Hi, sweetheart!" he yells into the house.

He and Jessica are always calling each other love names. I am embarrassed for them. They have no idea how ridiculous they sound.

We are greeted by the Blob making odd gurgling noises at the top of his lungs. The gray streaks in Jessica's long brown hair look like they have multiplied. Her eyes are red and her face is creased in places I had not noticed creases before.

Sam drops the grocery bags on the floor. "Is he okay? Are you—"

The Blob lets out a loud sound. "Maaaaaa!"

Sam's whole body jolts. "Is he—is he—"

Jessica nods jerkily. Then she breaks into a smile. "I think he's starting to talk. He keeps looking at me and saying 'Maaa.'"

Sam makes a breathy, moany sound like the Blob and gives Jessica a big bear hug. He sits down on the floor next to the Blob and starts banging pots with him.

Jessica wipes her eyes. "We've been banging pots all day. He bangs, and I say 'pot.' I'm sure he knows what I mean. When I pick up the blue pot, I even say 'blue pot,' and I think he knows what I'm saying. He's trying so hard to talk, but he can't quite make the sounds. Yet."

"You're doing such a good job!" I do not know if Sam is talking to Jessica or the Blob.

The Blob even laughs, I think, although it sounds strange. He waves the blue pot at me. Sam is chuckling and sniffling at the same time.

Jessica, still smiling, rubs her head with one hand, opens the cabinet with the other, and takes down her mega-size bottle of aspirin. That is what she gets for encouraging the Blob to speak.

"Be careful what you wish for, huh?" I say.

"What?" She cannot hear me over the two blobs banging their pots.

I head upstairs but Sam's big feet are following me.

"Hey, Matt? I was wondering if you'd like to play a game?"

I turn around and look at him. He looks like a fat little kid on the playground who wants to play Red Rover.

"A game?"

"Yeah!" He is still smiling.

Why is he not at work? I am thinking life must be a game for him, and then it comes out of my mouth. "Life?"

His smile fades. "I—I don't have Life." He smiles again. "How about Pictionary? That's a lot of fun!"

He does not get it.

"Uh . . . I have homework."

"Oh." He looks like his whole day is ruined.

"Maybe another time," I say, although I do not really mean it.

"Okay." He moves his head from side to side as if trying to get jolly again. He turns to go back downstairs, then stops. "Do you have any interest in woodworking?"

Woodworking! "Not really."

"Oh. Okay." His face looks deflated but he does not give up. "You wouldn't believe that I'm a pretty good shot at basketball, would you?" He grins.

"I did not know that. No."

"Well, I am. So, if you want to play sometime, let me know."

"Oh-kayyy." I draw it out, hoping he will get the point. Enough already.

He shrugs and smiles. I turn to go up the rest of the stairs.

"Matt?"

"What?" I try not to sound as exasperated as I feel. I have to be careful because they might be the types who say, "We can't help you, so you better go somewhere else." And there is nowhere else.

Sam stands there swinging his arms stiffly at his sides. His smile is gone. His brow is creased. "I want us to do something together. I—I want us to get to know each other better. We could go bowling or—or whatever you like. Think about it. Okay?"

"Okay."

He smiles a little like maybe he has broken through. I wish he would not try. It is not worth it. People just get hurt. It is better to leave things alone, Sam.

I make it up to my room before I hear Jessica say, loudly, "Oh, no! Look at this mess!"

I freeze and listen, even though it could not have been me. I have not been here long enough to ruin anything. Yet.

"Whoa, I don't believe it." It is Sam this time.

The Blob starts to moan.

I hear taps on the keyboard from the kitchen, and Sam's voice. "The office of Scottie Merrick, candidate for state senate, was found splattered with what police believe to be pig's blood. A spokeswoman for Merrick's campaign confirmed this evening that the candidate has received threatening phone calls targeting her lack of support for the war effort. Local police, the FBI, and the Department of Homeland Security are currently investigating the incident."

"Maybe they'll actually sit up and take notice," Jessica says, a hard edge to her voice, "now that a public official is being attacked."

"Well, you know what our chief of police says." Sam's

voice is still soft. "The attacks are so random it's hard to figure out what's going on. It doesn't look organized. Or
maybe it is organized, and the attacks that don't fit the norm
are copycat attacks. It could be kids—except for those inci-
dents that have happened during the school day. That's the
problem with terror tactics. You just don't know when or
where it'll happen next."

Jessica makes a sound halfway between a sigh and a
whimper.

The Blob moans again.

"It'll be all right, babe," Sam says.

I am not sure about Jessica or the Blob, but nothing
about this sounds all right to me. And I really do not like
having that peace flag hanging outside.

That night, the Blob will not shut up with the moaning
and I believe I have caught Jessica's migraine. I wrap my pillow around my head to drown out the moans. No luck. I try
stuffing tissues in my ears but that is not successful, either.
Maybe it serves Jessica and Sam right to have to suffer his
moans but it does not serve me right. I did not ask for the
Blob to speak.

"Shut up, dork!" I finally yell from my bed. He actually
stops, and I breathe a sigh of relief.

Then he starts again.

"Shut up, dork!"

He stops briefly but then continues.

"Shut *up*, dork!"

He does not stop.

I hear footsteps up the stairs. Jessica pops her head in.
"Language, please, Matt."

"I am speaking English," I inform her. "The Blob is speaking early Baboon."

It is dark, so I cannot see her expression, but I am sure it is not friendly. It may not even be Christian. "He's starting to speak, Matt. It's a wonderful thing."

"For whom?"

Moans from the Blob.

"I'm sorry, but you'll just have to deal with it."

"Can I go to a hotel?"

"No."

More moans.

"Maybe I will end up with some other relatives soon." I say it loudly. I do not know why.

"No."

I sit up in bed. "What do you mean, no?"

Moans.

"We like having you here." Her voice is sweet. I assume she is channeling Jesus, except that Quakers do not appear to be Jesus freaks.

I lie back down. "That will not last."

"I think it will. We just have one hurdle."

I am not sure I want to know about the hurdle. I finally decide not to ask.

But she answers, anyway. "We need for you to be happy with us."

Excuse me? Apparently, she has misunderstood whatever Loopy said. My feeling is not a requirement. It never is.

"Good night, children," says Jessica. "Love you. Sweet dreams."

I do not have sweet dreams. I have nightmares of being

out on the street where a dark, camo-clad, tattooed figure keeps tripping me and laughing, then asking me if I am happy and laughing some more. It is an endless loop. I am looking all around the street but there is no bed to hide under.

I wake up quaking.

CHAPTER EIGHT

School provides no refuge. Mr. Warhead is morphing into Hitler. He has those same insane eyes. And he plasters his remaining black hair over the bald part of his head so it looks like he just stepped out of Adolf's Hairdressing Salon. The worst part is the Hitler mustache, although I do not believe he is intending to grow a mustache. I believe his nose hairs are growing down so far that they are creating a Hitler mustache. I wonder if that is how Hitler grew his?

He is continuing to teach us about world events, the way he sees them, at least. We are fighting in Iran and Iraq and Israel and God knows what other "I" countries in the "Middle Eastern Theater." We are sending them "I" messages. From what I can tell, the messages sound something like this:

I do not understand your culture.

I wish you people could just act normal—you know, like Americans.

I can help you get a McDonald's adjacent to your current encampment.

We are also sending them troops to show how serious we

are about our "I" messages. But the other countries are serious, too, and our troops are up to their "I" balls in unfriendly fire. Including Mr. Warhead's brother, who is some kind of contractor over there. Now I understand why Mr. Warhead hates "the Enemy" so much. What I do not understand is why Mr. Warhead's brother would put himself in danger voluntarily. Is it for the money? Because he does not really have to go. He is not even in the military, for God's sake.

Mr. Warhead hands back our quizzes on which senators support our troops. All of my answers are right, but he gives me a B. He draws a big red *X* over my heading, "Warmongers." I believe the term is a matter of opinion and does not merit being knocked down a whole letter grade. However, his face is so red when he slams the quiz on my desk that I would not bring it up even if I did talk to teachers.

But I close my eyes and reserve him a spot on the next one-way rocket to Mars. I am hoping it will leave soon.

He is generally displeased with how the class did on the quiz, so he announces another one.

The screaming marker bleeds the words on the board. *"Name the countries supporting the war effort."*

I give the very short list of nations and believe they are all accurate. But at the bottom I cannot resist writing, "Perhaps we should listen to the United Nations?" I spend the rest of the quiz time coloring in the gashes on my desk.

Leering at me, Mr. Warhead says that he does not understand why some people who call themselves Americans want us to get out of the "Middle Eastern Theater."

"I think," a girl's voice says, softly, tentatively, "some people want to be patriotic. They just don't want . . . you know . . . more soldiers killed."

The room goes silent as Mr. Warhead's face gets redder and his lips press tighter together.

I peek between the rows and see a girl with frizzy hair, like mine only lighter. She is slumped down in her desk, also like me.

Mr. Warhead's voice is steely when he finally speaks. "Susan, you need to understand that many Americans feel that not supporting the war undermines our troops. That's why you hear the saying *You're either with us or with them.*"

"Yeah!" The Rat pounds his desk.

Mr. Warhead smiles at him. There is applause from the Rat's fan club.

"Now," Mr. Warhead continues, "as we know, some people are pacifists—"

"You mean chicken-shits?" the Rat yells.

His Vermin snort their approval. If people dare to disagree, they are only making themselves Victims. I steal a look at Susan. Her head is down.

Mr. Warhead says, "Let's watch our terminology," but he is still smiling.

The Rat grins, pressing his lips together hideously, mocking Mr. Warhead. But Mr. Warhead does not catch him, as usual.

I do not find the Rat amusing.

Mr. Warhead folds his arms and leans against his desk. "There are those who are conscientious objectors, but they still help the war effort by being medics or serving in some other noncombat capacity."

"Chicken-shits," the Rat calls under his breath.

"Often their religion won't allow actual combat," Mr. Warhead continues.

"Oh, like the Amish, right?" the Rat says. "Well, we don't need their horse and buggies for fighting MIGs, anyway!"

More laughter.

He is so condescending.

Mr. Warhead shrugs. "And Quakers."

I shudder and grab my desk to hold still.

"The ultimate chicken-shits!" shouts the Rat. He convulses his body into retchings and writhings.

Everyone laughs. Even Mr. Warhead is smirking although he is shaking his head.

It makes me want to retch. I cannot stand the look of the Rat quaking. The tornado starts inside of me. If he does not like Quakers, then he will be after me soon. He is not sneering at me now, so he does not know yet. But sooner or later, he will find out that I live with Quakers and I will be guilty by association.

But I am not a Quaker, Rat.

I am only quaking.

That is a quaker with a lowercase *q,* and it does not count.

I run all the way to English. Mrs. Jimenez gives us a "flash fiction" assignment. It is a short story that we write "off the cuff," as she says. I write about a girl who toys with suicide. Successfully. I suspect Mrs. Jimenez will still give me an A. Even posthumously.

Madame assigns us a paper *en français.* We must write it in the existentialist style where life is random and absurd. We can pick our own subject. Hmm. A paper about Random Acts of Unkindness. Let me think about this for maybe two seconds. Ah, yes. The Rat. What a perfect subject.

I take my usual place in the restroom for lunch and open

my bag. There is not one, but two apples. There is a peanut butter and jelly sandwich. And a yellow packet. That is more than any one person can eat, particularly in a reeking bathroom. I toss the sandwich, save the apples, and take a closer look at the packet. Fig Newton. A small tornado starts deep within me. I am nauseous. It is not the cookie. It is the name.

Fran Newton was a sweet old lady. My mother's cousin. "Home" number three. It was hard to believe she was related to me. I think she actually liked me, although I cannot imagine why. Most people start out nice, but it is a temporary affliction. You know that at some time the niceness will end. Because, as in every tragedy, there is always a fatal flaw. Either they never really wanted children or they had three and could not handle more or having two girls the same age simply does not work or you are damaged goods even though it is not your fault and they are sorry but probably it is best if someone else handles you and God help them.

Fran Newton went on being nice for so long that I dreaded the end more and more. I finally had to escape her, before she escaped me. I had to be harsh. It was better for her in the long run, anyway. She was too sweet and delicate. Eventually, I would have disappointed her. I had to move myself on to "Home" number four.

Now every yellow Newton packet is like a packet of sunshine that will never be again and its brightness is too much to bear.

I wrap the Newton packet in brown paper towels and bury it in the trash. I leave the bathroom quickly. Even though it is odd to run away from a bathroom when you think you are about to throw up.

When I am at my locker getting ready to leave, I smell

it. The Rat and his lesser Vermin are crowded around his locker snorting and hushing each other. They do this by randomly kicking and punching whoever is snorting the loudest at any given moment. They are obviously drinking. I can smell the booze. The smell stings my nostrils and tightens my stomach. It is sickening.

The Rat looks up and sees me. He sneers before I can look away. "What are you staring at, freak?"

He shoves me against my locker door and the lock digs into my spine and I want to cry out but I do not, I just keep my head bowed, hoping that maybe if I am lucky he does not recognize me from World Civ, and I run away. To the bus. Fast. I am sure he is chasing me.

I find a seat near the front of the bus but far enough back so I am not the first thing he sees when he gets on. I am crouching, head down, so the Rat will not notice me here. The bruise on my spine is throbbing. Please, do not see me, Rat. I am not even here. I am far away.

In my head, I am sitting in church next to my mother. I am five. It is the first time I have been in a church.

We are not exactly a religious family.

I think Jesus H. Christ is the old deaf man with the cane and funny hat who lives across the hall because my father is always yelling his name at the top of his lungs, but Mr. Christ never comes. The big guy in the white robe at church seems to know Mr. Christ, too, because he is also talking about him. A lot. Other people in white are walking down the aisle with palm branches. I think they are building a fort and I sit forward to watch. But all I see is the big guy at the front of the church pouring things in and out of decanters. The audience is walking up to him and getting free samples. I am hoping it is ice cream but I know better. I sigh and tell my mother we picked the wrong day. Today's sample must be salad because the big guy is making salad dressing.

I hear her speak but I do not see her face. *Why didn't I look up?* Her voice is soft and sweet. "That is the sacramental wine, honey."

"Oh," I say, "like Daddy drinks."

There is silence for a moment. Her voice is not sweet now but I know she is not mad at me. "No," she says slowly, "your father drinks the sacrilegious variety."

I make it off of the bus without being attacked by the sacrilegious Rat.

CHAPTER NINE

Jessica corners me. She is folding laundry in the kitchen. She asks me if I want a snack or hot chocolate or, her favorite, raspberry tea. She asks me if there is anything at all I need. She asks me about school.

I tell her it is under control. I wish she would stop trying to be like a mom. It is not worth it.

"What about friends?"

For a split second I think of Susan from World Civ. If I were interested in friends, I might start with her. But I am too practical for that. I will be gone before long, anyway.

"I have no friends."

She stops and looks at me. "Doesn't that make you feel a little sad and lonely?"

"Jessica, may I remind you that I do not have feelings?" I do a fake smile.

Jessica does not. "Children can be very cruel, can't they?"

She is scraping at my gut, trying to pull the feelings out of me. But I will not let her. I simply swallow hard and shrug.

"Okay," she says, "what about boys?"

"They are toads." Or Rats.

She smiles and her skin is all crinkly around her eyes. "Better not kiss one. He might turn into a handsome prince."

"Not in this world."

"Someday it could happen."

"Not likely."

She smiles a faraway smile and folds one of Sam's sweat-shirts. "What if you meet someone like Sam?"

Oh, gosh, I have no idea. Run?

"You know, Matt, Sam wants to take you bowling or something that you might like to do."

"I know."

I guess she can tell from my voice that bowling is not on my list of top ten thousand things I am dying to do.

"Even if you went to the grocery store with him, he'd like that. He just wants a chance to talk with you and get to know you better. He grew up with all boys, and he lost his father early on. . . ." She rattles on for a while about Sam. It is Thursday and he is always out until after dinner, so I suppose she is taking this opportunity to talk on and on about him.

I look over at his computer. Stuck to the side of the monitor is a piece of paper with typed questions. It has always been there but I finally decide to read it.

Do you work to make your peace testimony a reality in your life and in your world?

Do you weigh your day-to-day activities for their effect on peacekeeping, conflict resolution, and the elimination of violence?

Are you working toward eliminating aggression at all levels, from the personal to the international?

I imagine it is the Quaker version of "What would Jesus do?"

I hear Jessica ask what I would like to do and I realize she must be talking about what I would like to do with Sam. "I—I am still thinking." I am also thinking how much I do not want to be seen in public, even a grocery store, with Sam in his dork hat.

"Okay." She sighs and puts his sweatshirt in the laundry basket. "Well, how about helping me with the rest of the laundry?"

I look at the pile of oversized Sam clothes in the basket. "I cannot handle laundry."

"Can you handle dirty underwear?"

"Excuse me?"

"All your underwear is dirty. If you want it clean, you need to wash it."

"You have been taking care of it just fine."

"I was, but now that you're settled, you can learn how the washer works."

Settled? I am never settled. "No, thanks."

She looks at me for just a moment. "It's your choice."

So, no lecture, no making me do laundry. But she does not bother to do it, either. I ponder this. I never stayed anywhere before where I had to do laundry. Maybe I was not there long enough. Maybe I was too young. Or maybe they did not dare ask. I suspect it was that. Well, I have to give Jessica credit for asking me, at least. And holding out on not doing my laundry even longer than I can stand my rank underwear.

That night, I tell her, "My underwear stinks."

"I'll show you how the washer works."

I roll my eyes but she does not get nervous or angry. She just shows me how.

Turns out it is not that hard to do laundry. When the washer stops, you throw the clothes in the dryer and push the button. I do not know why Jessica made such a fuss about it.

The only bad part is that the washer and dryer are in the dark, dirt-floored basement. As I take my clothes out of the dryer, all I can think about is someone jumping out from behind the furnace and I run up the steps, two at a time, nearly crashing into Sam at the top.

"Oh, hi, Matt! Come on in the kitchen. I brought you ladies something."

I follow him in. Jessica is sitting at the table with the Blob in her lap. He is chewing a book. *Green Eggs and Ham.*

I stop. I stare at the orange cover. I remember this book. I had this book. I can still see M-A-T-I-L-D-A in penciled letters on the inside cover, starting large and getting smaller because I ran out of room. I can still see the pictures. I can feel the worn corners of the pages. I can hear the *swoosh-crunch* of each page turning. And I remember my mother reading it to me. I can almost hear the words. I can almost hear her voice. And my voice. Talking with her. As if she is a part of me and I am a part of her.

"Matt?" It is Sam. "Are you okay?"

I look at him. Why is my throat sore? Why am I blinking? It is just a stupid book, for God's sake.

Jessica grabs my hand.

I step away and shake them both off. "I am fine. What is the big surprise you were talking about?"

"Oh, right!" Sam carefully takes a white paper bag out of

the pocket of his Michelin Man vest and puts it on the table. "These are for you two."

"Go ahead and unwrap it, Matt," Jessica says. "I've got my hands full."

Even as she says it, the Blob rolls around in her lap so much that the book falls onto the floor. I bend slowly and pick it up by a dry corner.

"I got that book for Rory," Sam says, "because it was my favorite when I was a kid." He grins.

Mine, too. I have to hold it for a moment before I hand it to Jessica.

I walk over to the table and open the bag. There are two newspaper balls inside. I unwrap one and soon hear a scraping sound. It is a small white porcelain box, round, with a lid, with little raspberries painted on top and around the sides.

"Raspberries!" Jessica cries.

Sam shrugs and smiles. "That one's for you because you love raspberries."

Of course. I will get the leftover one that nobody wants.

"Thank you, sweetie!" Jessica cries. "Come on, Matt, let's see yours." She is smiling like it is Christmas.

I sigh and unwrap the other newspaper ball. It is another white porcelain box. With apples painted on top. And apple blossoms around the sides.

"And that's yours, because you love apples so much."

I do not know what to say. How does he know how much I love apples?

"I hope you like it," Sam says quietly.

Finally, I can speak. "What is this for?"

"Well, it's a . . . knickknack . . . thingy. You ladies always need a place for earrings or—or whatever little treasure you have."

"No, I mean why are you giving these to us? Is it a Quaker holiday or something?"

Sam and Jessica laugh.

"Sam loves to bring home treats," Jessica says. "And I don't normally let him," she adds in an almost scolding voice, "but once in a while, it's very sweet."

Sam rolls his eyes somewhere between "aw shucks" and "give me a break."

I take my knickknack thingy upstairs. I sit at the foot of the bed and put it on my low dresser. And I stare at the apples for a while.

When I take the lid off, it makes a granular *swoosh-crunch* sound because the porcelain is not smooth or glazed around the rim. I put the lid back on. It is like putting the lid back on Pandora's box, trying to protect the emptiness inside.

I open the dresser drawer and feel around until I locate the half-eaten roll of wintergreen LifeSavers. I open and close the box several times before actually putting the LifeSavers in. But they do not fit. Even a half-eaten roll is too large.

Carefully, I peel back some of the foil, take out one LifeSaver, and put it in the box, slowly *swoosh-crunch*ing the lid back on. I start to put the LifeSavers back in the drawer and stop. What good are they doing me there? I lean across the bed and grab my backpack, open it, and find the secret inside pocket, the new home for my LifeSavers. Maybe they will live up to their name.

I go to bed early because I am exhausted. I look at my knickknack thingy before I turn out the light. I decide it is an acceptable addition to the room.

I wake up later and hear Sam reading to the Blob. The rocking chair in the Blob's room is creaking and moaning with every sway of Sam's large body. He reads several books about farm animals and puppies. It is almost amusing to hear him making all the barnyard noises and talking in his puppy voice.

"Now, Rory, I saved the best for last." I hear Sam take a deep breath. *"I am Sam. I am Sam. Sam-I-am. . . ."*

It is *Green Eggs and Ham*. At first, I am mesmerized. And surprised at how all the words come back to me. *That Sam-I-am.* It is soothing in its rhythm and familiarity. *That Sam-I-am.* And I am lulled by the comfort and strength in Sam's voice. *I do not like that, Sam-I-am.*

And then I remember how dangerous it is to go to that place. The place you think is safe. Because it is not. It is fake, and if you do not keep your wits about you, you may start to believe it is reality. And the pain, when it ends, is all that much worse.

I put my pillow and even my bedspread around my ears to block out Sam's voice but it does not work. His low rumble is coming through the wall, through the padding, and into my soul. I pull the pillow tighter but I cannot block him out. I squeeze so hard that my eyes are watering.

CHAPTER TEN

Mr. Warhead is so patriotic he is practically drooling red, white, and blue. The whole room is dripping in American flags. There is a flag draped over the front of his desk, like it is a coffin. There is a flag hanging from the whiteboard. There is a flag stuck in his pencil holder. There is a flag on his coffee-dribbled mug. The wall switch cover is a flag. The basket with books is a flag. His mouse pad is a flag. He wears a tie with flags and a flag pin on his lapel. I am sure that even his boxers have flags on them.

As if he does not have enough flags already, today several giggly girls give him an American flag they have crocheted. Apparently it is his birthday. The giggly girls are his cheerleaders. Mr. Warhead and the Rock-ets. I am ready to throw up. The man does not need any more flags. The place is flapping with them already. Why not give him what he really needs—nose hair trimmers?

At least the crochet flag puts him in a relatively good mood and he decides not to give us a quiz, so I am free to scribble on my desk instead. I am determined to make something good out of the black and blue scars but I do not know what yet.

Mrs. Jimenez assigns us a major paper in English class. She goes around the room asking us what book we would like to write about. People are choosing books like George Eliot's *Middlemarch,* Ken Kesey's *One Flew Over the Cuckoo's Nest,* and even Proust's *Remembrance of Things Past.* I select *Little House on the Prairie.*

There are snickers when I say mine. For the first time, Mrs. Jimenez looks at me without shrinking. She is smiling and actually looks into my eyes. Maybe she is happy that I will not outwit her. Maybe she thinks it is adorable that I am being Little Girl in the Big World. Maybe she is trying to see past my IQ. I look away before she gets too close.

I believe everyone should have to read *Little House on the Prairie.* It is a fantasy. Pure escape. The family is friendly and fuzzy and fake, but it is fun all the same. You just have to remember that it is fiction. Real people do not care about each other that much. Except perhaps Quakers. But they are an odd breed and are dying out, I believe. Except in Africa.

Mrs. Jimenez tells us that if we have any problems we should come to her.

I seriously doubt she can help me with mine.

At lunch, I go to the library to start working on my English paper. I surf for information on Laura Ingalls Wilder so that I know what I am talking about. I did not know that her books were quite so autobiographical. I am stunned, momentarily, until I realize that the part about the friendly, fuzzy family is still fake. It is poetic license. Fantasy. I am sure of it.

I look around and decide I should spend all my lunch periods here in the library. It is much more pleasant than the bathroom. I peek in my lunch bag. The school day officially improves from F-minus to F. Jessica put cheese in my lunch bag. I devour it when the librarian is not looking and wonder what I will say to Jessica. Maybe nothing. Silence gives consent.

While I am still on the Internet, Mrs. Jimenez walks into one of the library conference rooms next to my computer. She is followed by a half-dozen students. They do not look upset, so I assume they are not in trouble.

I go back to surfing until I hear her laugh. It is always a little odd when a teacher laughs. So I listen. The conference room door is open, after all, so I cannot help but hear.

"No, I really can't," she says.

I hear a chorus of "please," "aw, come on," "maybe if you . . . ," but everyone is talking at once.

Finally, I hear Mrs. Jimenez above the others. "I'm still new. Wouldn't a peace club normally have someone like a World Civ teacher as a sponsor?"

"Except we only have one, and he happens to be Franklin High's registrar for the Selective Service. Not exactly a peace candidate, huh?"

"Yeah," a boy adds, "and Mr. Morehead is definitely not normal."

There is laughter, but a girl halfheartedly reprimands them. "You guys, come on. You know why he's like that."

I know that voice! Susan from World Civ! The one with the frizzy hair. Like me. I wonder if—

The door to the conference room closes and I look over at it, surprised, as if someone has suddenly muted the TV.

"Hey," a voice behind me says, "if you're not using the computer, can you get off? I've got actual work to do."

I grab my stuff and leave. But I wonder what is going on behind the closed door. And why Mr. Warhead is the way he is.

But I do not wonder for long because soon it is the end of the day and the bus ride is hell, as usual. The Rat's greasy, stringy dark hair falls onto his desert army jacket. His skinny black legs stick out from the bottom of the jacket like two snakes that have been lulled into service holding him up and then died of shock when they realized who was looming over them. The Rat may be in camouflage but it does not make him blend in. His pointed-toe boots trip people coming down the aisle. He makes unsavory comments about one boy's mother. He describes the blemishes on a girl's face, loudly, until she is in tears. He gets up and struts farther to the back of the bus to avoid the "bawling bitch."

I am guiltily grateful that I am not the Victim.

In the Quaker kitchen, Jessica is putting groceries away. I notice she has two large hunks of cheese. I watch her put them behind the margarine tub in the fridge drawer. It is not much of a hiding place but it will work for Sam.

I hear the front door open. "Hi, family!" Sam calls. "How is everyone?"

He walks into the kitchen and the Blob claps for him. Jessica gives him a kiss and he practically steps on one of the grocery bags on the floor.

"Whoa!" he says, stepping back and then peering into the bag. "Hey, did you get me any cheese this time?"

She gives me a quick, crafty smile. "Uh, no."

I have to give her credit. She is not lying. She did not buy the cheese for him. She bought it for me.

"When am I ever going to get cheese again?" he asks with a pouty face.

"When your cholesterol goes way below 312 like it is now!"

"But my good cholesterol is high, too," he protests.

"Good thing," Jessica says, patting his puffy cheek. "It can go to work on all that ice cream you sneak when I'm not watching."

He sticks his hands in his pockets, slumps his shoulders, and sticks out his bottom lip. "You're a meanie," he says, sounding like a two-year-old, and I can tell that he is barely able to keep from laughing. "I'm going to go find a wife somewhere else." He starts backing out of the kitchen.

Jessica pulls a package of napkins out of a grocery bag and flings it at him. He catches it with a grin and they both start laughing as Sam rushes at her, grabs her, and kisses her, which starts the Blob laughing, too.

We sit down to dinner with the new napkins. Purple. Again, they clash with the décor.

Over our dessert of apple slices and nonfat cookies, Jessica tells Sam that Our Lady of Peace was attacked a second time. "I thought it had just been threatened before," she says. "Did you know there was already an actual incident?"

Sam glances quickly over at me like he has been caught and looks at Jessica. "Uh, yes, I did."

Jessica's mouth drops open. "Why didn't you tell me?"

We both look at Sam. He squirms and sinks in his chair, pulling on his bracelet.

Jessica puts her hand on his. "I don't want you to be in danger, honey."

"I won't be," he says, but his voice is a little too high and defensive. "Don't worry, I'll be fine."

Why would Sam be in danger? Our Lady of Peace is Catholic. He is not.

Jessica shakes her head. "I guess you heard about Park Street Baptist early this morning, right?" Jessica's voice is a little too high and offensive.

He looks down at his plate and nods.

What is going on here?

"Oh, Sam! What if—"

He squeezes her hand. "We're such a small group, we're hardly worth addressing."

"But we do a lot—you do a lot . . . like what about every Thursday night?"

Thursday? The night Sam comes home late?

He shrugs. "People think Quakers are just kind of . . . odd."

"No argument there," I say, putting a large piece of apple in my mouth.

They both turn to look at me.

What? I am simply agreeing. "Nothing personal," I manage to squeeze out through my apple wedge.

Sam chuckles and looks back at Jessica. "Honey, we have to move forward. We can't let this stop us."

Jessica sniffs loudly and covers her mouth.

I am about to ask where, exactly, they are moving to but the Blob starts crying.

"Oh, Rory," Jessica says, picking him up out of the high chair, "I'm sorry. It's okay."

Once she has him with his head on her shoulder so that he is facing the wall, she nods at us knowingly. "See?" she mouths, barely above a whisper. "He can tell we're upset. He picks up on our emotions."

Sam covers his mouth and his face is so crinkled in pain I am afraid he is going to start wailing louder than the Blob.

I look at the crying Blob and then at Jessica. "He probably has gas."

Jessica's mouth drops open.

"Seriously. Little kids cry because of stuff like that all the time. It does not mean anything."

"Oh, but it does, Matt. He always picks up on my emotions. When I cut my finger chopping potatoes yesterday, I cried out in pain, and Rory started crying, too."

"You probably scared him."

She shakes her head. "When I was cutting the onions for the casserole tonight, I started tearing up and sniffling from the fumes, and Rory immediately started crying and grabbing for me."

I shrug. "I am still not convinced."

She stares back at me hard. "You know how you run into things in your room first thing in the morning?"

"That would be the bed."

"And you usually let out a cry or—or—"

"A curse word," Sam says, chuckling.

"Yes, well, Rory hears you, Matt, and he moans."

"He moans all the time, Jessica."

"No, I mean he stops what he's doing, looks up at the ceiling where your room is, and moans."

Okay, that is a little freaky. I look at the Blob and the way his dark hair swirls in the back like the coasters I used to make by coiling yarn. Jessica gives him a kiss and pulls him off her and starts handing him to me. His big blue

75

watery eyes blink at me, and I notice how long and curled his lashes are.

I push my chair away and fold my arms. I am not ready for that. Please!

"Come, here, Rory," says Sam. "Everything's okay."

The Blob's tear-streaked face gazes at Sam's grinning one. He breaks into a smile when Sam takes him.

Jessica smiles, too. "And he's always happy around Sam."

The Blob makes his gurgling laugh sound.

I know Jessica is looking at me with "I told you so" eyes and I refuse to look in her direction.

After I go to bed, I hear the phone ring. Sam's voice, then Jessica's shrill reply. I run to the top of the stairs.

"Rabbi Sterns?" Jessica's voice is strung thin. "Is he all right?"

"He was knocked unconscious." Sam's voice is soft. "They were going after the synagogue and he happened to be inside. One of the bricks hit him in the back of the head."

"Is he going to be okay?"

"They think so." A pause. "Aw, honey, they weren't targeting him. They were just going for another house of worship."

"Oh?" Jessica's voice is shaky. "How can you be sure? You know how much he speaks out against the violence in the Middle East. He even worked on that white paper—" Her voice breaks off. A sob, muffled, I imagine, by Sam's chest. "When will it stop?" she wails.

I cannot make out Sam's reply.

"Oh, Sam! Who's next?"

The Blob is moaning now.

I hear the front door open, flapping fabric, and Sam's

voice. "Honey . . . Jessica . . . what are you doing with the flag?"

"I—I need to sew it up. It's ripped and it keeps"—*flap*—"catching"—*flap*—"on the door." *Rip.*

It is silent for a moment.

The door closes.

"I'm sorry, Sam." Jessica's voice squeaks, as there is more fabric shaking and flapping and then a soft thud and quiet. "But we have children now. We can't endanger them."

The Blob is moaning again, softly.

He is drowned out by Sam's loud sigh. "I don't like giving in."

"Neither do I!" She lowers her voice but I can still hear her. "Matt would say it sucks."

"Well, she's right."

"Yes, she is." Jessica's voice is more forceful now, but they are moving back to their bedroom and all I can hear is muffled voices.

I am grateful to Jessica. And relieved that the flag is gone. Mostly. A small part of me thinks we are victims, losers. I will ignore that part of me.

I open my trinket box. The LifeSaver is still there. I close it again, spinning the lid more than I need to so the *swoosh-crunch* will drown out the moans from the Blob.

CHAPTER ELEVEN

Mr. Warhead hands back our quizzes on which countries are helping This Great Nation of Ours bring Freedom and Democracy to the rest of the world. My answers are correct but he gives me a B again and has a fat red circle around my United Nations question. He does not answer it but adds a question of his own: "Do you understand Patriotism?"

Patriotism? Yes, I understand patriotism, Mr. Warhead. Do you? Here is my definition: Patriotism is being true to your country and what it stands for. That would mean not being a warmonger without first asking the tough questions, like, *What are we doing, anyway? Are we really stopping terrorism? Are we really helping anyone? Or are we making things worse? Oh, and are people allowed to say what they think anymore or do we all just have to Shut Up?*

But Mr. Warhead is standing right next to my desk breathing hard and I remember the first rule of survival, the raison d'être, and I bow my head, stare at the gouge on my desk, and Shut Up.

"Some of you," he says in his nasal voice—and I can feel his hot breath blasting down on me—"don't seem to understand our duty to the rest of the world." He stops speaking but continues to hover over me.

Why will he not move on, for God's sake? I can still feel his breath.

"So, I'm forced to assign you a term paper on how and why Our Nation has responsibilities to the rest of the world."

The class erupts in protests.

"Hey"—his hot breath blows out directly on my head—"don't blame me."

Everyone turns to me and the hairs on the back of my neck stand up.

"Thanks a lot!" a girl hisses. It is not Susan.

"Jeez, moron!" a boy's voice adds.

"You'll pay for this." And I freeze. It is the Rat.

I shiver. God, why am I so scared of him? What can he do to me, really? Other than beat me senseless? Why do I feel that he would? Because he reminds me of every bully I have ever known? Senselessly violent.

Mr. Warhead gives a little snort and I shudder as he walks away from my desk. Everyone else still stares at me, and the Rat's eyes impale me.

Out in the hall, I see the Rat with the Wall and I walk in the opposite direction until I hear Mr. Warhead call, "Come here!"

I freeze and wonder if I can get away with saying I did not hear. But I know he will only get redder and the war will escalate so I slowly turn around. He is leaning against his doorway and the Rat and some older boys are walking over to him. He says something to them. The Rat nods at

Mr. Warhead and leers at the other boys. They are guffawing and punching each other. Just as I am realizing that Mr. Warhead does not want to see me, he does. And he stands up straight and drills his steely eyes into me and I walk backward into someone before turning and dashing away.

In the library, I sit down at a computer and try to work on my English paper but I cannot get interested in it. I cannot even get interested in eating the cheese in my lunch bag. All I can think of is Mr. Warhead. And the Rat.

I hear talking coming from the conference room.

"Yeah," a boy says, "Rabbi Sterns. My dad knows him. I can't believe it."

"I know, isn't it awful?" It sounds like Susan's voice.

I lean closer to the conference room door.

"Scottie Merrick better watch out, I guess."

"No kidding."

"That's Catholics, Baptists, and Jews, so far."

"That's what you get for being pro-peace these days."

"I think," says Mrs. Jimenez, "I'd like to start attending those peace vigils downtown."

So she did decide to be their sponsor! She has more guts than I thought.

"Can anyone give me more info about them?"

"Yeah, Mrs. J, I can," a boy answers. "It was started by some Quaker guy."

"Quaker?" I say it at the same time as Mrs. Jimenez.

"George Fox, maybe," he says.

"George Fox!" Another boy laughs. "Dude, that's the guy who started the Quaker religion, like, three hundred years ago!"

Laughter.

George Fox? The original Quaker? *George Fox?* I am intrigued. I decide to look up George Fox for myself. I am sitting at the computer, anyway. It is not much effort.

And I am shocked. Even though he was born in England way back in 1624 in a town called Drayton-on-Clay—can you imagine?—I actually like this guy. For one thing, according to all the drawings I find of him, his nose is easily as large as mine. And he was absolutely, brutally honest—which is apparently a Major Quaker Thing, according to this website—even when people were offended by his honesty or it was not socially acceptable. Ha! He saw through people and felt like a mature adult even when he was a kid. Ditto. He could not believe how hypocritical people were, especially so-called religious people. Bingo. And he was totally against organized religion. I hear you, George. He thought no one should tell him when or where to pray or bow to authority. Score more points for the Quaker boy! Also, from what I can tell, George never really had a "Home." The story of his life goes something like this: run out of town, beaten, run out of town, terrorized by countless Rats, run out of town.

I think George and I would have had a lot to talk about.

I am almost late to French because of Googling George. Madame returns my existentialism paper with an A, but her flowery words on the last page say, *"Mon dieu! J'espére que nous n'avons pas quelqu'un comme 'le Rat' à notre école!"* Well, you can hope, Madame, but unfortunately, we do have a Rat at our school. Watch yourself when you go out in the hall.

Or the parking lot. When I go out to the bus I see the

Rat and the boys who were talking to Mr. Warhead earlier. Except for the Rat, they all look like seniors. Boy-men. Misfits. All part of the Rat's Wall. I do not look directly at them. But I can see them out of the self-preservation corner of my eye as I walk to the bus.

They are smoking and I hear one of them say, "Dude, don't look now but isn't that your old man?"

The Rat ducks, turns, and steps back in one swift motion, his arm in front of his face, cowering. His panicked eyes flit around the parking lot. He is desperate, frightened, shaking.

And instantly I know why the Rat is the way he is.

And where he heard the word *chicken-shit*.

And why he uses it on others.

But it is still no excuse.

The rest of the Wall guffaws.

Without warning, the Rat punches one of the Wall in the stomach, hard, and the guy staggers backward, his hair in his eyes, trying to laugh but obviously struggling for breath. "Joke . . . man . . . jeez!"

I do not find any of it funny. However, I cannot help but peek at them through the window when I am on the bus. Why I feel the need to look is beyond me because I am nauseous enough as it is. The Wall is crumbling into the large, dirty sedan. I see the back of the Rat's head before he disappears. Staring at the filthy car, I cannot help but read the bumper stickers.

Peace Is for Sissies.

Pave the Middle East.

Remember: Pillage Then Burn.

When I want your opinion I'll beat it out of you.

Never settle with words what you can settle with a flame thrower.

The car peels loudly out of the parking lot, leaving puffs of black smoke behind.

Back at Casa Quaker, Jessica is on the computer. She says she is "working." I cannot remember what her job is, although I think she told me. Obviously, she works from home. Sam says he needs to look something up as soon as she is done. Why? He seems to have no job. Except Thursday nights.

I ask if I can use the computer after him so I can start on my term paper for World Civ. It is a mistake.

Sam is all excited about Mr. Warhead's term paper, "The Role of Our Great Nation in the Middle Eastern Theater." He shows me many websites. No one has ever tried to help me with my homework like this before. No one has even showed an interest.

I find it annoying.

I stare at him, hovering over me, racing the mouse around the globe on his "We Are One" mouse pad. I sigh loudly. "It does not need to be detailed. This teacher is not very bright."

Sam smirks. "Well, even if your teacher isn't, that doesn't need to stop you, does it?"

I roll my eyes.

He opens several windows and selects some more bookmarked sites. "Look, here's a site on Muslim women today. And this one's got stories of American soldiers who've been involved in the war and the effect it has had on them and their families. This is one on Islamic beliefs."

I stare at him. Why has he bookmarked all these sites, anyway?

"Well, doesn't it make sense to understand their point of view first?"

I speak slowly, as if I am talking to a very large version of the Blob. "Sam. Listen to me. We are being taught the American point of view only. I do not believe the teacher thinks these people are allowed to have a point of view. I am not even sure he thinks they are people."

Sam chuckles. "Maybe you'll be surprised."

I shake my head. No, Sam. You are the one who will be surprised.

"Aw, come on, give it a try."

I give a large sigh. "Fine, Sam, fine." If I play along, perhaps he will leave me alone.

I spend a long time doing research. Not because I need to. I could write the paper in an hour. But the websites are, well, interesting. Some of Sam's bookmarked sites are actually quite helpful.

He even has a blog! I am not lurking. It happens to be open and—surprise!—there is his picture. Why he posts his photo and real name, especially considering the sensitivity of being a "peace-monger" these days, is beyond me. Obviously, he never took "Internet safety" in school.

He seems to know a lot about the Selective Service system and conscientious objectors and where are good places to stay in Canada. I look because it could be useful for my future. But it is mostly about peace contacts and how to help the peace movement and how you will miss out on a student loan and a government job if you neglect to sign up for Selective Service—which I did not know—and does not specifically address how I can live in Canada with no actual family or money.

Still, it is interesting enough that I am surprised when Jessica says it is dinnertime already. When we sit down to eat, I realize I am starving. And that dinner is spinach balls. I cannot believe it. Up until now I have avoided them, but apart from applesauce, that is all there is on the menu.

Finally, I take a bite of a lumpy, green spinach ball. They are actually not bad.

"Have you thought about some activities you'd like for us to do together?" Sam asks me.

"Uh . . . I am still thinking." In truth, I had not given it a thought.

Jessica saves the day by talking about how the Meeting House is going to serve as a homeless shelter during the week and does Sam think people will be safe there? I am thinking it is probably no more dangerous than being on the street, but what do I know? She also says she is getting a ride to and from Meeting tomorrow because she is teaching a special session of First Day School.

First Day School is Quaker-speak for Sunday School. Imagine how awful that would be—having a First Day of School every Sunday.

And then it hits me. The Meeting House. Meetings. What a great way to spend time with Sam. Not the First Day School—God! But sitting in Meeting where we are not supposed to talk. I will not have to converse, and who cares if people see me with Sam in his dork hat there? They are all Quakers, after all. Jessica wears a brown corduroy shirt over her limited assortment of drab turtlenecks. I strongly suspect Quakers do not know what fashion is.

85

And it will keep Sam from helping me with my homework because I will remind him that we already have an activity that we share.

It is perfect.

"Sam." The conversation stops and I realize I am interrupting. "I was just thinking of an activity we could do together."

He puts his fork down. "Yes?"

"I would like to start going to those . . . you know . . . Meetings."

He smiles. "Really? Every First Day?"

Oh. I was not planning on that. But I suppose a onetime anything would not be enough and he is looking for some regular activity. At least I did not have to go the last several weeks. "All right."

"That's great!"

He and Jessica stare happy Quaker-speak at each other while I eat spinach balls and savor my victory.

CHAPTER TWELVE

I am regretting my brilliant idea of going to Meeting with Sam. Apparently, he thinks I am having a spiritual awakening. He does not know that attending Meetings is simply the least of various Sam-induced evils.

As we drive to the Meeting House, Sam says he wants me to feel "comfortable" in Meeting. He is enjoying giving me information about Quakers.

I am enjoying giving him a hard time.

"Now, Matt, if you have a concern, you can offer it up in Meeting."

"You mean like a sacrifice?"

He smiles. "No, I mean someone might pick up on your need and stand up and say something helpful."

"Like speaking in tongues? Or Quaker? I may not understand them."

Sam smirks at me. But it does not stop him. He tells me about the persecution of George Fox. I pretend I have never heard of the guy. "About three hundred and fifty years ago, George Fox started the Religious Society of Friends."

"Who are they?" I ask.

"Friends—that's another name for Quakers."

I suspect they came up with that name as self-defense so

that if they were accused of being Quakers, they could say, "Oh, no, we're just Friends." No one can hear the capital *F.*

We are a few minutes early, and as we enter the Meeting room, Sam gives me a monthly newsletter. I start reading it because it is another excuse not to speak, especially in front of a room full of religious types. And it is much quieter than a newspaper. The newsletter says that next month's topic is the Testimony of Tolerance, whatever that is, and this month's topic is the Testimony of Peace. Testimony? How do they come up with this stuff?

A man wearing a "Teach Peace" T-shirt clears his throat. "Does anyone want to sing a song before Meeting? Since we often don't get around to it after Meeting?"

I send him an "of course not" with my eyes.

"Sure, Chuck!" Sam says. And Sam runs off to a bookcase in the corner and grabs about a dozen hymn books in one arm. "What do you want to sing?"

Chuck smiles. "I think we need 'Walk in the Light.'"

Oh, barf! What a name! This is going to be one of those weepy, old lady hymns where voices will start warbling and tears will flow and I will get depressed from the melody alone. Why are so many of these religious songs like that? If there is a God, I am quite sure He or She does not want to look down on the Maudlin Masses.

Sam is chuckling and puts all of the books back but one. "I guess we don't need books for that!"

Of course. It must be the morose favorite. Please let it be short.

Sam flips through the pages of the one songbook and brings it to me.

I sit on my hands.

He puts it on my lap.

I stare at it like it has cooties.

"Who'll start us off?" someone asks.

"I will!" says Sam.

There are smiles all around the room, the kind of smiles that adults give small children who are being sweet or cute.

I do not find it cute at all.

And then Sam starts. Oh, God, he is awful! The man is tone deaf! I have never heard this song but I am sure it is not supposed to sound like this. My suspicion is confirmed when others in the room join in and it sounds as if they are singing a completely different tune, although the words Sam sings are the same.

I look down at the words, trying to block out the sound, and I see George Fox's name. Since the lyrics are about George, I decide to read them. In the chorus, George walks off in his old clothes and "shaggy, shaggy locks." I imagine George running at full speed, tripping over his shaggy locks to get away from Sam's singing. Others in the room are singing cheerily, apparently unbothered by the Sam-blasting.

And then I realize something. It is not a morbid song. At all. In fact, people have started to ad lib to the chorus and clap a part of it. I imagine it is like being in camp. It is almost fun. Wait. Did I say "fun"? No, that was not me, truly. Anyway, the song is over now and the room buzzes with chatting and laughter.

Sam puts my book back and creaks himself down in the chair next to me again. "Did you like that?"

There is enough noise around that I can be inconspicuous. "Not bad," I say, because I am so relieved that it was not a maudlin hymn.

He grins and sits up straight like a happy puppy.

Oh, God. I did not mean him! He is awful. Someone should set the man straight. "I would not advise you to try out for *American Idol,* however."

He laughs, hunkers down in his chair, and winks. "I'll tell you a secret. I can't sing."

No! Really?

"But I love to. I just have to sing."

"Why? Is that a Quaker Testimony?"

He screws up his face to think, even though it was not a serious question. "Let's see. I was *honest* about my singing ability. That's one." He taps his chin.

I think of the newsletter I was just reading. "And people are *tolerant* of your singing. That would be two."

There is laughter. It is not just Sam's. And I realize that people are looking at me and smiling.

I quickly look down at the newsletter and read.

I discover that one of the missions of this Meeting House is to lobby the legislature to end the fighting in the Middle East. There is a website to contact your senator and representative directly. I also see an announcement about collecting school supplies for children in the Middle East whose schools have been bombed by one side or the other or both.

There is a tribute to Tom Fox, that Quaker peace worker who was abducted in the Middle East a while ago. I cringe, even without reading the article. I remember the event and that is enough. Tom Fox was brutally killed.

Finally, there is an appeal to attend the weekly peace vigils downtown on Thursdays from 6 to 7:30 P.M. Bring candles. Contact Sam Fox for more information.

Is every Quaker named Fox? Maybe they are all related.

Wait a minute! Thursday nights? The night Sam comes home late. Sam Fox? *Sam!*

I look over at Sam. His eyebrows raise. He looks almost alarmed. Perhaps he is reacting to my expression. I point at the Sam Fox in the newsletter and he smiles and nods. I do not.

I look away. I think about what Jessica said about that rabbi. Was he singled out? Are they starting to attack people now, not just buildings? I am not sure that these peace vigils are such a good place to be. Not that Sam would listen to me. I look over at him but his eyes are closed. I shudder because I realize that Sam Fox and George Fox and Tom Fox really are related, even if not biologically.

The room is silent. Meeting has begun. And it is freezing in this place. Heat must not be a Quaker Testimony. Perhaps this is a sneak preview of next month's Tolerance Testimony. You must build up a Tolerance for the cold.

It is quiet, except for people sniffing or taking deep breaths and exhaling or shifting in their squeaky chairs. The furnace starts with a boom and I shudder. Apparently, enough people have been praying for warmth that they have willed the furnace to start.

The woman next to me did not have breakfast. Or even dinner last night, by the sound of it. Her stomach is louder than the furnace. I wonder if the whole room can hear.

Oh, no. It is contagious. My stomach is talking to hers. It is worse than yawning because you can stifle a yawn even when everyone around you is doing it. I have no control over my insides.

Sam pokes me with his elbow and grins. Are Quakers supposed to grin in the Meeting room? I think not. So I scowl at him.

When the furnace shuts off, it is so quiet that it is like pure nothing.

I hear a cell phone chirp but no one answers it. No one even budges. The ringing continues. *Ring, ring, ring-a-ling, ring-a-ling, ring-a-ling, ring-a-ling.* Over and over. I am surprised that there is no sign about turning off cell phones and pagers. And surprised that it does not stop.

Then I realize it is a bird. Of course. Quakers probably do not own cell phones.

I do not know if it is my brilliant AP brain that finally figures it out or the bird's flicker that catches my eye. But I look at the bird out the window, sitting in a high branch and looking in on all of us. It stops chirping when it sees me staring at it. And stares back at me, cocking its head from side to side. It has black and white stripes above its eyes, much like my mascara. And yellow. It looks good on the bird. I am not sure I want to go there with my eye makeup.

I hear a snort next to me and whip my head over to Sam. He is grinning at me and glances up at the bird.

I scowl again and cross my arms. So I am distracted by a bird. This does not exactly make me ADHD. There is, after all, nothing going on in this room.

I decide to look at the other people. And I notice their fashion non-sense: white socks with black shoes, a striped skirt with flowered top, and a scarf so moth-eaten it is quite possibly a hand-me-down from George Fox himself. To be honest, though, I do not care what people choose to wear. Unless it directly embarrasses me. Like a too-small baseball cap.

A woman stands up, slowly, shakily. She is older than Jessica but not ancient. "I've been trying to make sense of it," she says, "but I still can't. He was my rock. Why did God take him?" Her lips are quivering and she closes her eyes and sits down but not before the tears creep out from under her eyelids.

No one says a word. They sit like statues, eyes closed, some sniffling but basically ignoring her. I cannot believe how cold they are.

Finally, people start squirming in their chairs and taking deep breaths and I know it is time for Meeting to stop.

Sam stands up, anyway. "I have some afterthoughts. Phyllis, I wish I had an answer for you. I don't know why Steve was taken. I've been thinking about it for the past several months myself. I never understand why things happen. Sometimes I get it later." He shrugs. "Sometimes not. For now, all I can say is you have us, and we're with you."

The people around Phyllis close in on her like a shawl, wrapping her in warmth, and others move over to occupy all the empty seats near her. Sam kneels in front of her and everyone is talking at once and the words weave a cloak around her and I realize that I am the only one sitting on my side of the room and it is me who is the cold one, not them.

Later, I tell Jessica about Phyllis. I do not know why. It is not my problem. But for some reason it bothers me.

Jessica immediately goes to the computer and starts Googling.

"What are you doing?" I ask.

"Finding a recipe."

I think this is an odd reaction to Phyllis's plight. "What on earth for?"

"I want to make her some Lamingtons."

"Excuse me? Is that some sort of Quaker treat?"

"No, it's a dessert she misses from her childhood. She says they just make her feel good. I've been meaning to make her some. She has terrible arthritis and can't do much with her hands. I hope the Lamingtons will give her some comfort and remind her of Australia."

"Australia? God, you people get around."

She wheels around on the stool. "Language, please, Matt."

Oh, for God's sake. Sam does not have a problem with my swearing. Why does she?

She glances over at the Blob. "It's a bad influence on Rory."

I roll my eyes. Like it could possibly matter. "Okay, okay, I meant *gosh*!"

Now the Blob is staring at me. And puckering his lips. And spitting. But a sound comes out, too. A new sound. While he stares at me. His little red lips form an O. "Awshhh, awshhhhh."

"See!" Jessica runs over to him. "He's learning! He's copying us!" She looks at me. "He's copying you, Matt. You said *gosh*!"

"Shit!" I cry, because I realize she is right. He is copying me!

"Matt!"

"Oh, God—I mean, shi—" I cover my mouth with both hands before more shit can escape.

CHAPTER THIRTEEN

Mr. Warhead stands at the front of the room and opens a large envelope as he announces another quiz. The class groans, but not too much because Mr. Warhead is an easy grader. Except when it comes to me. Still, I have memorized everything about our current warmongering, so I am thinking I am in good shape. Memorizing has always been easy for me. It is the forgetting that is hard.

I scribble some more on my desk, notice that the room has gone silent, and look up.

Mr. Warhead is squinting his gun-barrel eyes at me. "For this quiz, you will use your heart."

Now I know I am in trouble. Because I have no heart.

"You will defend our fighting overseas. Not with opinions, not with casual 'I thinks,' but with facts about what constitutes an American and what our responsibilities are, as a superpower, to protect the rest of the world."

He moves away from the board and I see what he has just tacked up. It is a large photo of a dead marine.

His body is splayed out in an awkward fashion, on his back but with one arm twisted underneath him in a very unnatural way. His other arm is on his gun. There is red all over his chest and stomach and you know there is nothing left intact. His eyes are open in that fixed stare of the dead. Above his eyes are a few short curls of hair stuck to his forehead. Like the Blob.

I have to look away for a moment or I think I will throw up. I swallow and take a deep breath. When I look back again, I see someone in the street in the background. Also fallen. Also dead. I know who she is. Her white head scarf partially covers her face and her hands are reaching out because she did not want to die because she has a child who needs her. I cannot take my eyes off her.

"You have twenty minutes," Mr. Warhead says sharply, and I jump. How did he get here? Next to my mother. Who is slumped on the gurney. With the sheet partially covering her face. And her hand, limp and cold, dangling out from under the sheet. Reaching for me.

I look around me—everyone is writing furiously. I am feeling hot and cold at the same time. And nauseous. I stare at the blank piece of paper on my desk. And the photo on the board. And every time I look up and see the slain woman my eyes fill up so much I cannot see the lines on my paper, so it is impossible to write anything even if I could think of something to say.

"Time's up!" Mr. Warhead announces, and he walks around the class collecting the papers.

The bell is ringing and I clutch my paper and slowly get up, too slowly because Mr. Warhead is standing in front of me. He grabs the paper out of my hand before I can escape.

"Just a minute, young lady!" he sputters. There is spit shooting out of his mouth. He clenches his teeth and wrinkles his nose as if my paper stinks. "Let me tell you something." He looks up from my paper and grinds his gun-barrel eyes into me. "I'm tired of your flippant remarks and bad attitude. I spoke with your guidance counselor. You know, you're not the first AP student I've taught. Just because you're a little smarter than the average kid, don't think you're exempt from work. You'll be getting an F. This will definitely have an effect on your grade this quarter. You'd better watch yourself or you'll end up failing."

I do not answer and stagger out into the hall but my heart is pounding. I have to pass this class. And he is the only World Civ teacher. There is no getting around him. He can destroy my chance to escape to Canada. To graduate early. Maybe even to graduate at all.

I start down the hall to biology and see the pointed-toe boot too late. My palms hit the linoleum with a slap and I am sprawled on the floor. I can smell the smoke of the Rat above me and hear his snickering. I scramble up as fast as I can and run past a blur of pushing, laughing, and shouting.

When I round the corner, I slow down enough to catch my breath. As I walk, I realize that I am sore, but I am not dead. I can survive the Rat. I am still shaking, however. I think it is partly rage. How dare he get away with treating people like this?

And I am enraged by Mr. Warhead, too. How dare he threaten me like that? Sure, I know how to pass his class. I can become the kind of perfect "Patriot" he wants to see . . . like the Rat. Ha! That will never happen, Mr. Warhead. Do not count your chicken-shits before they hatch. I will die before I become a Rat.

What am I saying? Why do I care? What difference does it make, anyway? I should just give Mr. Warhead what he wants, and then, hopefully, I can get what I want.

I pass the Armed Services posters by my guidance coun-selor's office and think of the Dead Marine photo and stop and shudder. I look through the front windows of the school and see the snowstorm that has started. The snow is falling thick, heavy, with occasional swirls that twist in a dizzying, sickening pattern. It snowed just like this the day they told me my mother was gone forever. I remember that now. The snow poured out of the sky, whiting out everything. And I am not sure who cried more, the sky or me.

Back at Casa Quaker, Jessica is stirring a pot of soup on the stove. She is the only person I know who makes soup from scratch. It comes in cans now, Jessica. I believe Napoleon started that trend for his troops a few years back.

She looks at me, her eyes squinting. "Are you okay?"

I do not know how to answer this question. Is there any-thing at all about me that is "okay"? I do not bother to answer.

The Blob is saying his "awsh" noise and standing against the cabinet under the sink. I look at him because it is un-usual for him to be upright on his own. He mistakes my look for interest and grins, reaching for me.

I step back, into Jessica. She strokes my hair and I pull away. It is not worth getting close. It will all get whited out in the end, anyway. When I go to Canada. I think.

She sighs. "It's hard being fourteen, isn't it?"

I am not so sure about that. I am thinking that being four and hiding under the bed to escape my father's boots was tougher than this. Five was bad, too, having to go off to kindergarten, leaving my mother alone with the Beast. Did I ever do anything to help her? No, I just hid like a little dork.

But six was the worst. When I got off the school bus, and the police cars and ambulance were in front of the apartment. And I knew it was my mother. I tried to push through all the people but they refused to budge. When they finally looked down at me, they all stepped back so I was in the middle of a big empty circle. Everyone went silent and they looked like they had just eaten something bad and felt sick. They were staring at me, alone in the spotlight. Finally, the guy I thought was Mr. Christ pulled off his funny hat and hobbled over to me and tried to kneel down next to me, but his knees cracked so much, he bent down instead. He smelled of mothballs and oranges. His cheeks shook and I saw the tears streaming down the wrinkles in his face, and I screamed because I knew my mother was in those tears.

The next thing I remember, a lady in a white uniform told me my mother had gone to heaven. I kept wondering why it was taking her so long to get back from that place. I wished she'd gone to Wal-Mart because it had everything you could possibly need. Then I wondered if she had to go grocery shopping, too. Sometimes the lines there took forever. She should have picked the IGA. It was quick and the checkout lady always gave me a lollipop.

I had heard about hell from my father. In fact, he told us to go there on numerous occasions. I knew it must be a bad place. But I never knew what heaven was. Grown-ups talked about it like it was special. After a while, I decided heaven must be a place like Disney World where people go on vacation. I was mad at my mother for going on all those rides and not taking me with her. Finally, I stomped my foot at some grown-up and asked her if she had any idea when my mother was due back from heaven. She said never.

When I got older I decided that heaven is really the same thing as hell. It just has more vowels.

CHAPTER FOURTEEN

I t is First Day again. For some reason, it seems to come around more often than Sunday. Jessica and the Blob go downstairs to First Day School and the play group afterward.

I grab a newsletter and sit down on a creaky metal chair. I am beginning to recognize some of the regulars in Meeting. Like Phyllis. Like the man who wanted to sing last week, Chuck. And the woman next to him. Laurie, I think. Their names are in the newsletter. They are always holding hands.

Sam sits next to me in the quiet Meeting room. He swallows. Loudly. I glare at him but his eyes are closed. It is amazing how noisy a swallow is in a silent room. And how much you feel the need to swallow, too, when you hear it.

I am focusing so hard on preventing copycat swallowing and keeping the saliva in my mouth that I think I might choke.

I look down and peruse the Quaker shoes around me. Old, peeling running shoes. Dirty boots. Sandals with socks. They go well with Sam's cap.

I am still trying not to swallow, so I read an article in the newsletter I picked up in the hallway. It is more about the

Peace Testimony and why war is not the answer. And there is a line from the George Fox song we sang last week. "You can't kill the devil with a gun or a sword." I want to show the article to Mr. Warhead. Or leave it on his desk when he is not around. Maybe if a Quaker came to school, if they do that, someone could disarm him. Or at least make him see the other side of the story.

I jump when a woman's voice cracks through the air. "I'm sitting here pondering our commitment to peace," she says, "and thinking how we, as Friends, should put ourselves out there more, like at the schools, to get students—and teachers—thinking about peace."

Oh, my God, it is like Sam said! I must be thinking in Quaker. It must be this room. My thoughts are running around and planting themselves in people's brains without their even thinking! Like an Immaculate Perception.

I see the woman sit down and realize that she just finished speaking and I missed the rest of what she said. Because I am still in shock that somehow my brain waves are broadcasting in Quaker. I am not sure if this is a good thing or frightening.

I hear the cell phone bird and look out the windows trying to find it. The sun is streaming in and I realize that it is warmer in the Meeting House today. Finally I see the bird peeking in at me. I am actually enjoying the sound the bird is making. And the fact that I can sit here undisturbed.

I watch a man hunched over, elbows on knees, head hanging, eyes closed. And the younger version of himself next to him, maybe a college kid, in the same position. And I realize they look similar not just because of their shape but because of their faces. They must be father and son. And I wonder what it must be like to pray with your father instead of pray against him.

When Meeting is over, a woman stands up and looks at Sam. He smiles back. She says we have decided to introduce ourselves after Meeting. I am thinking this is silly, considering it is the same people every week. How can they possibly not know each other? Even I can recognize them after only coming here a few times. I am also thinking that since I had no part in such a decision, I can just slip out the door, but Sam's hand closes on mine and pulls me back to my chair. He stands up, still holding my hand so it is dangling in space. I look away, trying to divert people's eyes from my conspicuous arm.

"Good morning." Sam smiles and looks around the room. "I'm Sam Fox."

"Ohhhh," someone says, exaggerated, chuckling. "Haven't I seen you somewhere before?"

Another chuckle. "You mean, like, here?"

"No, I was thinking at the peace rallies on Thursday nights."

"Oh, yes, I think he's been there . . . once or twice."

More friendly laughter.

Sam gives a wry smile, then squeezes my hand and looks down at me.

What? I say with my eyes.

He tugs at my arm a little and his eyes answer. *Aren't you going to stand up?*

I shake my head and look away.

He coughs. "This is Matt."

There is a chorus of "glad you're with us," "welcome," "hello."

I can feel my face burning and my arm tingling.

"Matt's fourteen and she goes to Franklin High. She's in the ninth grade, but she's mostly taking classes with the juniors and seniors because she's a very smart young lady."

For God's sake, Sam, they do not need to know my entire life history!

"She's part of our family now. We hope she'll be with us for a long time." He squeezes my hand again and smiles at me and I wish he would just let go.

There is an awkward silence and finally Chuck stands up and introduces himself. Sam sits down and loosens the grip on my hand. I let out the long breath I have been holding inside.

As soon as the circle finishes the recital of names, I run for the front hall and am the first one out the door.

I hear the steady *clump-clump* of Sam's boots coming down the Meeting House steps behind me. He must realize that I have had my fill of socializing and it is okay to leave now because he does not call me as I head down the street toward the Subaru.

Suddenly, I hear sharper, quicker footsteps getting louder. I turn and see a man storming up behind us. He does not look like a Quaker. He looks angry.

"That sign is an insult!" he shouts, pointing to the peace banner on the Meeting House.

I step behind Sam.

"It's not meant to offend—" Sam begins.

"My son is over there fighting, and you idiots are back here hanging signs like this while he's risking his life for your goddamn safety!"

I am torn between running away to save myself and trying to pull Sam with me because he obviously does not know he should run away now.

"I understand," Sam is saying calmly, "and I appreciate what your son is doing, believe me."

I stand with my arms folded and my head pointed down. It is like saying "shut up" without moving your lips. It also keeps my hands from shaking because I do not like angry men yelling at me or anyone. I have heard that when you are part of a crowd in a play and you are supposed to be making background chatter, you say "rhubarb, rhubarb, rhubarb," and it does the trick. I am wondering if saying "rhubarb" in my head will also cover up the angry man's voice.

Rhubarb, rhubarb, rhubarb.

The rhubarb does not work.

I hear Sam's voice clearly. "I don't believe our safety was at risk—"

"You're poisoning your daughter's mind!" the man is yelling. "Hey, girly!" The man tries to step around Sam, but Sam is too quick for him. And I am glad of Sam's size.

"Matt, go to the car," Sam says quietly.

I am too scared to look up. Or move. I feel the tornado inside me. And my whole body is shaking. All of a sudden, I realize that I am surrounded. By a wall of legs. And I almost scream. Until I see the shoes. Old running shoes. Dirty boots. Socks in sandals. These are Quaker legs. Attached to Quaker bodies who enclose me like a Quaker Cloak and shepherd me. Toward the Subaru.

I am inside the Subaru but the Quaker Cloak still surrounds me. It parts only when Sam opens his door and joins me.

"Everything's okay," he says. "We just needed to talk it out." He looks at me. "Are you all right?"

"Are you crazy?"

He stops putting the key in the ignition. "What do you mean?"

"Did no one teach you to run from bullies? Not confront them."

"Aw, he wasn't a bully, Matt. Just an upset father. And I don't blame him." He starts tugging at his silver bracelet. "We . . . we agreed on a lot of things. I explained why my feelings . . . run so deep." There is a catch in Sam's voice and his face goes red. I wonder what he means but he coughs quickly and goes on. "It was a good opportunity for us to understand each other, to tolerate each other."

"It was also an opportunity for disaster. For God's sake, Sam! Why not talk about peace somewhere safe, like a school, instead of talking with crazy people on the street?" I exhale loudly. "What if Jessica is right? Maybe they are targeting actual people now, not just buildings. Like that guy— Rabbi Sterns? You could be in danger."

"I'm not a rabbi."

"But you are—"What is Quaker for rabbi? Un-Minister? Chief Fox? "—the Alpha Quaker."

Sam shakes his head and laughs. "Alpha Quaker?" His whole stomach is shaking.

"I am not joking!" He is so annoying. "What are you going to do if that guy comes back again?"

"Probably the same thing I'm already doing."

"Which is?"

"Hold him in the Light."

"Excuse me? Is that like holding his feet to the fire?"

Sam chuckles. "No, it's, well, it's like praying for him." He stops smiling and clutches his bracelet. "And for his son."

I shake my head. "I still think you are playing with fire."

He turns and looks at me. His voice is quiet but unyielding. "Sometimes you have to face the fire, Matt."

I shake my head and look away. That is where I differ with the George Foxes and Tom Foxes and Sam Foxes. It is unwise and unnecessary to stick your neck out like that. Speaking out loud. In public. You will not find me in that position. Not in a million years.

CHAPTER FIFTEEN

Late that night I wake up because someone is playing a guitar downstairs. And singing. It cannot possibly be Sam because this man's voice is actually in tune, and it is definitely not Jessica. Finally, I realize it must be the radio or a CD. It could not be the TV. Although they have a small one in the kitchen, it is only decorative. They never turn it on.

I get up and creep quietly to the top of the stairs. I am not trying to spy. But the singer sounds soft and serious, especially in a dark, quiet house.

I sit on the top step and listen for a while. The brown carpet is thin and does not provide much padding, but at least it is warmer than no carpet. I pull my nightshirt around me and lean against the stairwell wall.

Music drifts up from the kitchen. The refrain is ripping at my gut.

When you're losing your heart,
When you're losing the fight,
Hold on to my hand,
And we will follow the light.

He is saying that I am lonely and lost and I wonder how he knows. And he says to follow my heart. But I have no heart. So how do I know where to go?

I get up to go back to bed because I cannot stand to hear him say it one more time. I stand there for a few moments, though, because the strange singer has some kind of hold over me. It is as if he is singing directly to me. I shudder, because it is a spooky thought.

And then the singer stops. I hear a Sam sigh and the wheely stool sliding across the kitchen floor, then heavy footsteps to the living room.

After I hear the creak of their bed, I wait a few minutes and tiptoe down to the kitchen. By the light from the computer screen, I see some CDs on the kitchen table. They are all by the same singer, John McCutcheon. I have never heard of him. Probably because he is an old guy. He must not be a total fart, however, because he does have pierced ears. Otherwise, he looks like someone's father. But a nice one.

I pick one up and look at the titles of the songs. My throat hurts when I read the one called "Follow the Light."

Others sound funny. I open up the CD and read the lyrics from some of the songs and they are hysterical. Or very true. Like "New Kid in School"—"The first day is a hundred hours long" and "Everything I do I know is wrong."

I notice something shiny by the computer. I put the CD lyrics down and step over to the light. It is a large bracelet and I realize it must be the one Sam wears. I pick it up. It is made partly of chain links with a large, rectangular metal piece that stretches across the middle, joining the chains. On the metal rectangle is engraved PVT. JOSEPH L. FOX. Underneath his name is a date, 7-1-72. I stare at it for a full minute before I figure out what it is.

I drop the bracelet on the floor like it has burned me. It

falls with a clatter and I scramble to pick it up, as if picking it up faster will erase the noise it made. But I knock the wheely stool, sending it crashing into the fridge and bouncing off again. When I grab it to stop it from moving, I lose my balance and stumble over it, sending both the stool and me crashing to the floor.

"Shit!" I say, not quietly enough.

Sam is in the doorway in red sweatpants and a blue Superman T-shirt. I imagine Jessica gave it to him.

"Um, hi," I say, from my spot on the floor.

I hear Jessica's sleepy voice. "Sam, is everything okay?"

"Yes, honey. I'll be there in a minute. Just getting a drink." He bends down and reaches his arm out, to help me up, I suppose. But then he sees the bracelet on the floor and picks it up instead.

"I was just looking at it. And I dropped it. Sorry." I set the stool upright.

He is staring at the bracelet, rubbing his thumb over the name and date as if trying to wipe some dirt away, even though it is shiny. Sighing, he creaks himself down on the stool, still staring at the bracelet. He looks so serious and sad, I say "sorry" again.

His head pops up like he has heard me for the first time. "Oh. That's okay. What are you doing on the floor?"

"I . . . I heard that music earlier and I was looking at the CDs and—"

"John McCutcheon. He's my favorite artist. Quaker, too."

A Quaker? This is not my image of a Quaker. I stare at Sam. "Are you sure? He has pierced ears, for God's sake."

Sam nods. "Yup."

"And he—he's *funny*, for God's sake."

Sam smiles. "Yup."

"And he—" and then I realize the Quaker connection. "And he sings antiwar songs."

Sam loses his smile and stares at the bracelet. "For God's sake."

I look at the floor for a while, then I watch Sam, who is still staring at his bracelet.

"Is that . . . someone related to you?"

He nods. "My dad's MIA bracelet. He was a medic in Vietnam. My mom wore it until she died. Then I inherited it."

"Is the date . . . is that the date he died?"

"No. It's the date he went missing in action."

Missing in action? What does that mean? Was he ever found? I try to remember what Jessica said about Sam losing his father but all I remember is tuning her out. I make a mental note to start listening to what Jessica says. It could be useful.

I look at Sam, thinking to ask him more, but I stop when I see his glistening eyes. I think maybe he is going to cry. I want to tell him I am sorry but it sounds so inane. Sorry that your dad got killed or tortured halfway around the world for God knows what reason. Sorry that you lost your dad, who probably actually loved you, when you were just a little kid. Sorry you had to grow up without your dad. Sorry your whole life got screwed by having to be a grown-up before you had a chance to be a kid. Sorry.

Now I see that Sam is looking at me. "Well, honey, I shouldn't keep you up any longer. You have to get your sleep so you'll be alert for school." He tries to smile, but it looks sad. "I don't want you blaming me when you don't get into the college of your choice—except I hope you choose one close to home. Of course, we'll come visit wherever it is, but it'd be nice if it weren't too far."

I look down at the floor. That depends on how far you consider Canada to be.

"In fact, I'd like it if you stayed here during college, but Jessica says that you'll probably want to go off to college. That's part of the college experience."

They have actually talked about this? I thought people only planned for their kid's college in commercials or, at the very least, when they actually had kids. I steal a look at him to see if he is serious.

He shrugs. "Okay, you can go wherever you want. I can tell you agree with Jessica. I should've known. Just not too far away, all right?"

I feel like I am in some strange movie, only I am the stand-in actress and no one has given me the script. "I—I will think about it."

"That's my girl."

I tell myself I will look into cheap flights to Canada. Then I tell myself to stop being so stupid. Surely, Sam and Jessica will lose interest before then.

I look up and Sam is leaning over, extending his hand.

Slowly, I reach and his huge, warm hand envelops mine. How can it feel so soft and so strong at the same time? He pulls me up, holding my hand and squeezing it gently, even after I am standing.

"Good night, Matt. See you in the morning."

"Good night."

He is still holding the bracelet of death as he wobbles away, looking like an overgrown kid in Superman pajamas.

I pick up the CD lyrics and look at them one more time.

> When the world feels so big
> And we seem so small
> And you wonder if life
> Has any meaning left at all...

My throat is closing and my eyes are getting like Sam's, so I criticize the song's meter, throw the lyrics on the table, and run.

CHAPTER SIXTEEN

The Dead Marine photo is still hanging up in World Civ.
I cannot stand to see it. So I scribble on my desk instead.
Mr. Warhead is pacing up and down my row, lingering as he turns at my desk. I can feel his heat. "It always surprises me when girls can't see the importance of helping oppressed girls in other countries. Sure, it's okay for you here, but what about women around the world? Think of what they have to go through. Don't you owe them anything?"

I grit my teeth and squirm in my seat. Of course I care what they go through. For example, I would rather they not be in the middle of a war zone. Being injured or killed.

"Yeah, I'm doing what I can," the Rat says. "I'm signing up."

Mr. Warhead is at the front of the row and he nods. "You'll get your chance soon enough."

"Maybe sooner," the Rat answers, under his breath.

"It's good to see that some of our young people care," Mr. Warhead says.

I let out my breath. Too loudly. It is not a snort, not a cough, not even a sigh, but just a slight sound. Of disgust. And it is all the Rat needs.

He turns slowly in his seat. I sink behind the boy in front of me, but suddenly my shield ducks down to get something out of his backpack and I am exposed. Staring straight at the Rat.

"Chicken-shit," he breathes.

My stomach churns. Loudly. And I cannot stop it. I think of Meeting. I imagine the Quaker Cloak around me again and I imagine that the Rat's eyes cannot penetrate the Quaker Cloak.

All day I manage to avoid the Rat and I think I am protected by the Quaker Cloak, even when I get on the bus. It is a stupid and dangerous mistake.

Without warning, the Rat has my backpack in his grimy paws. I feel like the Cloak, and a part of me, have been ripped away.

I start to shake. It is the only thing I know how to do. I do not know how to retrieve my backpack from the Rat when I must avoid him at all costs.

"Here, dude!" He throws my backpack across several seats to one of his Vermin.

The catcher laughs. "Whose is it?"

"Ma-til-da's!" The Rat laughs at the sound of my name.

When it gets thrown back to the Rat, he tosses it to the other side of the bus.

Hands and greasy heads seem to pop up all over as my backpack is hurled around the Bus from Hell.

"Let's look inside," the Rat says, and I think I will throw up.

The LifeSavers! They cannot take my LifeSavers! My arms fly up in the air before I can hold them back down again.

But the Rat notices. He has my backpack. "What's in

114

here, huh?" He unzips the main compartment and I shudder. I try not to look. I try to block it all out. My eyes are clouding over. I hear the noise of many people on the bus, not just the Vermin. They are laughing and talking. How can so much noise be so empty?

I see my math problems flying through the air. I see an apple. Also mine.

"Ooooh, look, a secret com-part-ment!" The Rat draws out the word, stretching out my agony.

I do not know if I can stop the tears. I cannot stop the squeak.

"Hey, Matilda the chicken-shit is trying to talk! What is it, huh? The secret compartment?" He puts his hand on the zipper, shaking it, grinning. "What's in here that's so important?"

I say the first word that pops into my head. The only thing that might stop a fourteen-year-old boy. But my jaw is stiff and I whisper the word so softly, so as not to squeak again, or cry, that I cannot even hear my own voice.

Suddenly, his face is beside me. "Speak up, moron!" he yells in my ear. The entire side of my body prickles into goose bumps and I shrink away.

I whisper it again.

"What?"

I turn and look at him. His face is all blurry. I can smell his rancid breath.

"Tampons," I hiss.

He drops my backpack on the floor.

"What did she say?" one of his Vermin asks.

"Nothing! She's a mute, remember?"

"Toss it here, then!"

"Nah, she's a freak. There's nothing in there I want to touch."

The Rat is in his seat, laughing with his Vermin, so I quickly bend down and grab my backpack, clutching it to me, as I rock back and forth.

The next stop is mine and I stumble out into the falling snow. Its whiteness covers the dirt and the slush and the gray. Its blanket deadens the world's sounds, sucking the cries out of babies' mouths. But it can never soften the fear or the pain.

CHAPTER SEVENTEEN

Jessica does not ask if I am okay after school. Even though I am shivering. And sweating. And about to throw up. She is too giggly and pink-faced about her own news. "Guess what? Sam got a job!"

I am still reeling from the Rat, but the significance of what she says finally hits me. "You mean, he did not have one already?"

"Well, he was doing community service."

"Community service?" My knees start to buckle so I sit on the floor, still clutching my backpack, and narrowly miss the Blob. "To pay for what?"

"No, no, not forced community service. Repairing houses for the elderly. Working in the drug rehab clinic. He also reads to prisoners. He volunteers because he wants to help our community."

"Oh, you mean because he cannot get a real job?"

Her pink face is turning red now. "He's working on his GED."

"He never even finished high school?" I am surprised. Sam is definitely not stupid. I know that now. He probably knows more about what is going on in the Middle East than Mr. Warhead, for God's sake.

Her mouth is closing into a tight-lipped line. The pot on the stove starts to bubble over. The liquid hisses as it hits the burner and cooktop. Jessica turns a knob on the stove and grabs a napkin—blue-flowered—again, they clash with the décor. She dabs at the spilled mess. Not very successfully, I might add.

Her voice is shaky, like she is trying to rein in her words so they will not come out screaming. She stares at the pot on the stove and stirs it deliberately. "You know, Sam had a lot of people depending on him from the time he was a young boy. His father died when he was only five, and he was the oldest of three kids. By the time he was eight, he was mowing lawns, raking leaves, shoveling snow, anything to make money. Because he was so responsible, he started babysitting when he was eleven. As a teenager, he didn't have time to focus on school. . . ."

The Blob is grabbing for me and I slide across the floor. He slides after me. When did he get to be so quick? He does not crawl but sits on his butt and yanks on chair legs or anything handy to pull himself along. His hands reach out to me, opening and closing rapidly. I decide to stand up. In time to hear Jessica say, "So he's going to be a substitute bus driver."

Excuse me? Is this Sam's new job that Jessica is all excited about? I review the school hierarchy in my head:

Student
Coach
Teacher
Principal
Guidance Counselor
Librarian
Nurse

Cafeteria Worker
Custodian
Substitute Teacher
Bus Driver
Snake on the Football Field
Substitute Bus Driver

"Substitute bus driver?" I ask. On what bus? The Bus from Hell?

Jessica smiles at me like I am finally seeing the light. "Yes. He even gets to start tomorrow because he already has a bus license from driving a bus for special-needs kids last summer. Now there'll be two lunch bags in the fridge, so I'll put an *M* on yours and an *S* on his, okay?"

She is way too excited. I think about my bus ride home. I need to set her straight. "It is not a nice job, Jessica."

Her smile disappears.

"Someone should inform Sam so he is not completely humiliated."

Jessica does not appear receptive to my help. In fact, her narrow face gets even tighter as she sucks her cheeks in. She slams the spoon on the rim of the pot and stares at me with squinty eyes.

I am startled.

"I wish you wouldn't say things like that about him! He's a very sweet, caring person." She is breathing heavily and her face is blotchy red. "And what's more, Sam really *cares* about you!"

She turns away and looks at the pot, stirring furiously.

I turn away, too, but I have nothing to look at and nothing I can do. I want to tell her that I was not intending to be obnoxious. I am only trying to help. Now I am too

119

stunned to say anything. I go upstairs to my room and pon-der her statement. *"Sam really cares about you!"* Is she sure? I cannot decide if I want her to be right or wrong. It is so unnerving when someone cares. So complicated. It is almost easier if no one cares.

I slump down on the sofa bed and drag the sheet over my head. I pull the LifeSavers out of the inside zipper pocket of my backpack. I finger the roll. Amazingly, no LifeSavers feel broken. It is not a weakness to carry them with me. Some people carry dead animal parts, politely referred to as a rabbit's foot. That is disgusting. LifeSavers are normal.

I refuse to chew them up and watch them spark, like Sam said, however. That is not normal. And my LifeSavers would be gone.

I hear Sam come in. Jessica and Sam whisper downstairs for a long time.

"No, I'll go talk with her," Jessica finally says.

I hear her footsteps coming up the stairs and I put the LifeSavers away in their home.

She knocks at my door.

"Yes?"

"Um, it's Jessica. Can I come in?"

I pull the sheet off my head and shrug. Then I realize she cannot see me. "All right."

She opens the door slowly, as if I might throw something at her. Her eyes are red. "I'm sorry I lost my temper—"

"It does not matter."

Her eyes look even more pained and she closes the door behind her, leaning against it. "Yes, it does. I shouldn't have yelled at you."

It is something to talk about other than "caring," so I go with it. "I thought Quakers were not supposed to get hostile."

Jessica sighs. "I'm not a natural at this, okay? I wasn't born a Quaker. Sam was. He never seems to react with hostility. He rarely even raises his voice."

"He is an odd man, that Sam."

She takes a deep breath.

"But not in a bad way," I add quickly.

She smiles and sits down on the sofa bed next to me. "He's a real sweetheart." She starts grinning like the girls at school when anyone of the Blond Male persuasion looks at them. Her cheeks are even getting pink. She looks at me, losing the girlish grin. "And he really does care about you, Matt."

The *C* word again. I squirm.

"He wants us to be a family."

I am picking so hard at the chenille loops on my bed-spread, I am surprised they are staying intact. I blink and swallow hard. And I change the subject. "So, how did you guys meet?" Women always like to tell the story of when they first met their man.

"At the legal aid clinic."

My eyes are open wide and I sit up straight. "Which one of you was in trouble?"

She smiles. "Neither of us. I'm a lawyer, remember? I work there, usually from home now, because of Rory. Anyway, Sam came in for some advice on a project he was handling."

"Oh, right. Lawyer." Now I remember.

"I did tell you."

"True, but I was no doubt ignoring you."

She squishes her lips into a pout but her eyes are smiling. "No doubt."

There is an awkward pause. I do not know what to say so I go back to picking at the loops on the chenille bedspread.

"Matt?"

I look at her.

"We really want you to be happy here with us. We—we've tried to have children, but I keep having miscarriages."

"Perhaps it is a sign from God that you are not meant to have children." It sounds nasty, which I do not mean. I am so bad at this. She is blinking hard, so I explain, "Children are a hassle. Maybe God is saving you the trouble."

"Or maybe it's a message that we're supposed to take care of the children who are already here." She smiles at me.

I look away again.

There is a knock at my door and I jump. My heart races.

Sam's voice says, "Is everything all right in there?"

Jessica turns to the door. "Yes, honey."

My heart is still pounding. I am thinking of the times my mother and I sat on the bed like this with the door closed. And the chest of drawers shoved against the door. While we held each other. Listening to the banging on the door. Hoping that my father would not break through.

More knocking.

I jump again. My breathing is fast and loud. I cannot help myself. This is the part where my mother helps me scramble under the bed.

"Hey, guys," Sam says, "I got some ice cream at the store."

Jessica smiles, closes her eyes, and shakes her head.

"It's raspberry ripple."

Jessica is still shaking her head.

Another knock.

I cannot stand it anymore. "Will you stop banging on the door, for God's sake?" It comes out loud and screamy. That is not how I mean it.

Jessica's mouth drops open. Her forehead is pinched and she is staring at me.

"S-sorry," says Sam slowly, sounding like a hurt little kid.

This is what always happens. People do not understand my behavior. Then they get hurt and confused. But why can they not see it from my standpoint? The creature on the other side of the door was always a Beast. All of a sudden, now he is supposedly a man who Cares? How can I click so quickly to a new reality? And truly believe it is real? And believe that it will stay real?

Late that night, I still cannot get to sleep. I keep playing with my knickknack thingy, taking the lid off, looking at the LifeSaver, putting the lid back on with a *swoosh-crunch,* then lifting it again to see if the LifeSaver is still there.

Finally, I get up and sneak down to the fridge. There are two brown paper lunch bags inside, one with an *M* and one with an *S*. The *M* bag is already obviously smaller than the *S*. Still, I open up *M,* take out the Ziploc bag with my hunk of cheese, and put it in *S*.

I hear a creaking sound from the living room, which is Jessica and Sam's bedroom. I freeze, then frantically shut the fridge door to stop the light inside from shining up the entire kitchen. Jessica would not be happy to know that Sam is getting cheese for lunch tomorrow. But I know it is not

Jessica's cholesterol phobia I am worried about. I am worried that someone will see what I am doing. Giving something to Sam.

But then I remind myself. I am only paying him back for the LifeSavers. That is all.

CHAPTER EIGHTEEN

I cannot get away from the Photo of Death. It is not only in World Civ now. It is in the library. Slapped partially across the top of the peace club sign on the conference room door. As if the photo itself is not enough of an affront, someone has scrawled words coming out of the dead marine's mouth: Are you with us or with them? An arrow points from the words to the peace club sign.

My stomach is full of acid and I swallow hard to keep it from rising. I have some ideas who put the photo there. It is the Rat or the Wall or Mr. Warhead. They are all Beasts. The embellished photo is so sickening that I am spurred into action.

I am glad it is the weekend because I decide to write my term paper for Mr. Warhead from the Middle Eastern perspective. I am a Middle Eastern woman whose village has been bombed by the Unified Forces of Freedom and Democracy, otherwise known as the United States. The Middle Eastern me has lost her entire family. It is easy to be the Middle Eastern me. I picture the soldiers as the Rat and the American Government as Mr. Warhead. I name the Middle Eastern me Fatima. Fatima is a very angry woman. She invokes a curse on all of the Rat-soldiers for their tongues to fall out so they can no longer speak evil and for their fingers to curl up so they can no longer hold weapons. Nothing happens to their feet, however, so they are free to walk home.

I am in Fatima mode, typing my term paper, when Jessica tries to interrupt me. I am too busy to listen to her. Fatima is flattening out dough for bread and watching the fire. She throws a handful of rice in the pot of soup. While she makes dinner, she sings, thinking about the time she threw flowers at the American soldiers because, at first, she thought they were peace makers. They said they were bringing democracy. She is still waiting. The soldiers are still here, but instead of democracy there is more fighting and so many innocent people are dead, including children. Fatima's thoughts are too important to be interrupted by a little Quaker woman who needs a gallon of milk.

"Matt, did you hear me?" It is Jessica, still trying to break through.

"Yes." But I am more interested in what I am writing. "Milk."

"And Rory."

"I know."

"Is that okay?"

"Yes." Just go.

"I'll be back in a few minutes, then."

"Fine."

I hear her jangling her keys for a moment before her footsteps make it to the door and out.

Silence. Finally.

"Maaaa."

I whip around on the swivel stool. The Blob is sitting on

the floor, clenching and unclenching his fists, staring at me. I catch my breath and rely on my exoskeleton to keep me calm. "Oh. Right. You are here. She said that."

His eyes look questioningly at me.

"Do not expect me to be a babysitter. I have no experience." He is still looking at me. "I have never babysat before. I do not know what to do."

"Maaaaaa!"

"She is not Ma. She is Jessica." He should not get too attached. That would not be wise for a foster child. "And," I add, "she is gone."

His eyes register something. Is it confusion? Is it panic? Or is that mine?

He moans, as if he is going to start crying.

"No. Do not panic. She will be back. Soon." I look at the clock on the stove. It is covered with crud but I can read the time—11:18. However, the crud seems to be slowing the second hand down to a crawl.

"Maaaaa!"

"Her name is Jessica. And she is not a very good housekeeper." I pick up a napkin from the pile on the counter. It is pink. Apparently, variety is more important to Jessica than matching the décor. I start wiping the scrapple and other crap off the clock. I scrub so fast that I bang my knuckles on the stovetop. Hard. Then I scrape them on the knob next to the clock, the knob that has a broken jagged edge, so my knuckles are bleeding.

I take another pink napkin and shove my knuckles into it. The Blob is sliding himself across the floor toward me. I back away and bang into the stove. I look at the clock. It is 11:19. And 27 seconds.

The Blob is reaching for me. "Maaaaa!"

"She is not here." My voice is shaking. "Go . . . play."

He looks at me with his big blue eyes and curly eyelashes as if I am an idiot. He is right. He cannot go play. Quickly, I go to the cabinet with the dented pot. Jessica's grandmother's. The Blob's favorite. It is not there.

I bang the other cabinet doors open and closed, looking everywhere in case Sam put the dishes away and the pot ended up with the mugs. The pot is nowhere. The Blob is moaning. The clock is not moving.

Dishwasher! I pull the door open and rummage around the bottom rack for the small pot. Sam believes you can put a thousand items in a dishwasher and, as long as you turn it on, everything will get clean. No pot.

I push the dishwasher door closed, lean my chin on the counter above it, and groan. Like the Blob.

The dish drainer! Right in front of my nose. I yank the items out, throwing them in the sink as I go.

"Maaa!" The Blob is pulling on my skirt now.

There it is! I pull the blue pot out and hand it to him so fast I almost hit him on the head. "Here!"

He looks at it as if it is some foreign object and does not let go of my skirt. "Maa!"

I drop the pot on the floor. It has failed. I am starting to shake now. I look at the clock: 11:21. I cannot handle this much longer. How long can it take to pick up some milk?

The Blob has found my bloody napkin on the floor and is trying to pull it apart. I pick up a fresh napkin and start shredding.

11:22. Where on earth has she gone for milk?

The napkin does not occupy the Blob for long and he

starts wailing. I pick up several more napkins and continue shredding.

11:24. Is she finding her own cow?

The Blob is pounding the floor with the pot, crying.

11:26. Do not be so picky, Jessica. Any cow will do.

There is a pile of pink snow on the counter. Along with the bloody pink snow on the floor.

11:29. You said "a few minutes," Jessica. It is more than a few minutes.

The Blob is banging the pot against his head. I grab it away from him. He screams.

11:30. How could you do this to me, Jessica?

I cannot take care of other people. They will fall apart if left anywhere near me. Like my mother. I did nothing to help. Nothing.

The Blob grabs for me. I run out of the kitchen and up the stairs, two at a time. I get to the top landing and hear him scream. I want to go up the last three steps and disappear. Go in my room. Shut my door.

He screams again.

I cannot look into his helpless fawn eyes. It is easier to make him stay the Blob if I do not look. I clench my teeth and turn around.

The Blob is dragging himself up the stairs with his hands, leaning backward as he does, like a tightrope walker who is about to plunge to his death.

"No! Stay!" I put my hands out like stop signs and shake my head. It is not difficult. I am shaking so hard already.

He keeps coming. He is on the fourth or fifth step. I try to go down the steps but my legs are shaking too much. "Do not come any farther!"

His "Maaa—" turns into a scream. His eyes look at me with fear, pain, love, hate. The way my mother looked at my father.

He tumbles backward and lands with a thud at the bottom, a tiny lifeless form with one of his arms bent behind him in a very unnatural way.

I am a murderer! I am not just passive death, I am an active murderer! I run down the steps and my legs collapse under me. I am falling, tumbling. Steps and ceiling. Steps and ceiling. I hope I die before I hit the bottom. It will serve me right.

Instead, I am lying with my face on the floor, looking into his. Are we both alive or both dead? I do not know. His eyes are closed. And then he groans. Dead people do not groan. He is alive.

I know better than to move him. I am not an idiot. I start to get up to call 911 and I stumble down again because my head is still upside down and I am dizzy. The front door opens and hits my head, which is now in the way.

"Oh, my gosh!" It is Jessica's voice. She is kneeling down next to me. "Matt, are you all right? Rory!" She leans over him. "What happened?"

"I fell." An obvious and stupid thing to say.

"I'm calling 911!"

"I was just going to do that," I say, trying to get up again.

But Jessica makes me lie still. She thinks I have a broken neck, apparently. I tell her I am fine but she is refusing to believe me. She only says, "Thank God you're all right!"

So I thank Him. But I also ask Him why he bothered.

Within moments, I hear the siren screeching. I hate ambulances. I hate the way their lights cut into your head. I hate the way their sirens pierce your soul. I hate the way they took my mother away.

"What happened?" We are in the hospital waiting room and Sam is staring at me. His eyes are not mean or angry. But they are serious.

So I tell him. About the clock and the moaning and looking for the pot and how that did not work and not knowing what to do. I stop then. Because I do not want to tell him about running up the stairs. Trying to run away. But I know I have to.

"I—I ran up the stairs and he started climbing the steps after me—"

I hear his sharp intake of breath so I hurry on.

"I did not know he was following me, at least not at first, so I ran—"

"You can't always run, Matt."

He puts his hand on mine and I shiver so convulsively I throw his hand off. But his huge hand comes back and closes around mine and holds it, not tightly, but firmly enough that my shuddering cannot get rid of him. And I look over at the waiting room door.

"You can't run and pretend things aren't there."

That is what I always do, Sam. And it works. Well, usually it does. I know he will argue with me, however, so I say the only thing I can think of and it comes out whiny and wailing and there is a catch in my throat and I do not know why. "I did not know what to do."

He squeezes my hand. "I understand that," he says softly, "but running away won't help."

Jessica comes to the door and we both stand up.

"How is . . . the kid?" I ask. I cannot bring myself to call him the Blob.

She smiles. "It's okay. He just had a mild concussion. He'll be fine."

Sam walks over and hugs her.

My arms are crossed so tightly that my hands hug my shoulders. And I do not know why I want to cry.

"We'll be right out," Jessica says.

Sam sits down again and tugs on his MIA bracelet.

I sit down, too. I am too exhausted to stand.

"Matt?"

I look over at Sam. Now he is gripping his hands together like he is praying. "You can't run away from things because then you can't change them. You give up your chance." His blue eyes bore into me. "And then it may be too late."

Too late for what? And what chance is he talking about? And why does he make running away sound like a bad thing? It is simply the fight-or-flight response. I will not fight. So my option is flight. Like going to Canada. I will be fine on my own. I am used to it. Really, it is easier that way.

CHAPTER NINETEEN

I t is First Day again. Jessica has a migraine and decides to stay home with the kid. After everything that has happened, I am actually relieved to be going to Meeting where I can sit in silence and everything is quiet and safe.

As Sam and I walk up the Meeting House steps, we catch up with Phyllis, who smiles at us. "Good morning, Matt. Good morning, Sam."

I am surprised to hear my name but Sam does not miss a beat.

"How are you, Phyllis?" Sam asks, taking her hand.

She sighs. "I'm all right. I do want to thank Jessica for those lovely Lamingtons."

"Oh, Jessica's not coming today, I'm afraid," Sam says.

"Well, will you thank her for me, please?"

"Of course, Phyllis."

Sam helps Phyllis take off her coat and hangs it on one of the pegs in the hallway. As I stand there waiting for him, several people come up to me and say, "Good morning, Matt," as if I belong here. There is a man with kind eyes behind his glasses and wrinkled face, and Chuck and Laurie, who walk in together and smile as soon as they see me, as if I am their friend whom they have missed seeing all week.

After an elderly woman clutches my hand and shakily says, "Good morning, Matt, dear," I finally remember to say good morning back. And I realize I know hardly anyone's name and perhaps I should ask Sam.

But he whispers a question to me before I have a chance to ask him. "What are Laming—whatevers?"

"Australian cookies," I whisper back.

His forehead is still crinkled.

"Phyllis's favorite from her childhood."

"Oh." And he looks at me as if he is surprised that I know something in his territory that he does not.

I am surprised, too, but it is the good kind of surprised.

I sit in Meeting and think about Phyllis and the Lamingtons. And Jessica. And the kid. Not that I want to think about what I did. Except that it all turned out okay in the end. I wish life were like that. I would not mind the fear and the pain if I knew things would turn out okay eventually. But I think about Mr. Warhead and the Rat and my life, and it seems unlikely.

I try to decide how to handle the fact that Mr. Warhead will probably fail me. I imagine my prospects for success are poor. And I am not sure how effective the appeal process is for a cynical student whom no one knows exists. I am an insignificant country battling the Mighty Warhead. It does not look good.

I do not even want to think about the Rat. Everyone in Meeting is calm and serene. The Rat is not exactly calming. So, I look at the quiet faces around me and think about what they might be thinking about. Their thoughts must be better than mine.

One of my counselors, the one I called Fish Face,

although not to his fish face, told me that I should let people see into my thoughts. If he knew what was there, he would not ask to be invited in. My mind is full of ugly and frightening things. I believe I am being altruistic to keep the ugliness inside. Why should other people have to see any of this? How can it help them to know any of my horrors? I do not wish that on anyone.

Even my best thoughts are not exactly pleasant. The only good thoughts I have are borrowed from books, like *Little House on the Prairie*. It would be better to go straight to the source. Telling Fish Face to go to the library and read some good books did not go over well, however. His face expanded like a blowfish.

Fish Face said I am selfish because I hide my feelings.

Fish Face was an idiot.

I hear my cell phone bird and peer through the windows. When I look at him, he chirps louder, more insistently, putting his whole body into it. And I stare back at him, not caring if Sam notices, because I am trying to understand. Because I am sure this bird is trying to tell me something but I do not know what.

Then, to my horror, I do.

Shattering glass silences the bird.

Sam yells, "Everyone down on the floor!"

I am there first. I know the drill.

Bricks and rocks are raining in on us.

He yells again. "Put your head under your chair!"

My head is already there.

Inside my head, there is screaming, my silent screams. Outside the Meeting House, there is screaming and yelling. But in between the inside of my head and the outside of the

Meeting House is a room of people who are still and quiet. All I hear is breathing, the click of a cell phone opening, and then a man's voice, not Sam's, talking calmly to the 911 people. He sounds as if he is ordering a pizza rather than ordering emergency vehicles. He quietly and briefly answers questions, giving more information, as if he is ordering more toppings for the pizza.

My head is tucked into my lap, under my hands, under my chair. I feel a hand on my back and I jerk up so violently that I knock my chair shelter over and I am exposed.

"It's okay, Matt, it's just me," I hear Sam say. I feel his Michelin Man arm come over me and feel his bulk like a wall around me. Better than a thin, metal chair. "It's okay, honey. We're going to be fine."

I hear the sirens and I pray that he is right. Sirens do not necessarily make everything fine. Where are the attackers? Why did they attack now, when they know people are inside? It is not just a building. It is people. Then I realize that there is no more yelling outside. And no more crashing glass.

Sam is getting up and is struggling to pull me up with him. I remain in a ball. Has he learned nothing from armadillos?

He gives up, but keeps a hand on my back as he talks to the police. I know they are the police because their radios keep barfing out codes. I do not know how they can listen to Sam and understand what he is saying when they are constantly interrupted by crackling dispatcher voices belching into the conversation.

Finally, they stop. I do not know for how long before

Sam shakes me a little. "Matt, honey, it's okay. It's over. Everyone's gone. Even the police."

I look up. The Meeting House is white and calm and quiet, as it usually is. Except for the broken windows and the yellow police tape blaring DO NOT CROSS THIS LINE.

Sam helps me up and walks me to the car, patting my hand most of the way, as if that will heal everything.

We drive in stunned silence. At least, I am stunned. Sam is more alert than I have ever seen him. His eyes are sharp and keen and his jaw is set. He drives steadily with just one hand, while the other pushes his curly hair back as if to say "enough of this childishness!" He is missing his cap. He looks like a completely different person.

I am sitting on my bed. I am not sure how I got here. I am clutching my LifeSavers. I can hear Jessica and Sam talking downstairs in hushed voices and the kid yelling for Jessica's attention, "Maaa, Maaa!"

Then I hear shuffling outside my door. "Matt?" It is Sam's voice. "Can I talk with you?"

I do not respond. My mouth is hanging open but I do not know how to make my voice work.

"Matt?"

I make a sound in my throat and a moan comes out of my mouth. I sound like the kid.

"Matt? I need to come in. I'm not going to knock, okay?"

The man is not an idiot.

"I'm opening the door now."

I look up at him, my mouth still hanging open. It is the only loose part of my body. The rest of me—fingers, arms, legs, feet—are wrapped around me like a contortionist. I am a tightly tangled fit of twine.

Sam leans against the door frame and stares into my eyes. It is not the stupid clown Sam. It is the no-nonsense Sam. "I'm sorry you had to go through that." He presses his lips together and starts yanking his knuckles and making them pop. Loudly.

The popping pulls me out of my stupor. Quickly. I am rapidly moving toward irritated and disgusted.

He rubs his MIA bracelet and lets out a long breath. "I know that must have been frightening for you."

Oh, no, Sam. It is a wonderful way to spend a Sunday morning. Under a chair. With rocks crashing through glass toward you.

"I know you've already been through some rough times in your life," Sam says.

I shrug. "So have we all, right." I do not say it like a question but he answers, anyway.

"No. A lot of kids have had very happy, sheltered lives, especially compared to you."

I stare at him. Enough with the Quaker honesty, already! "Is this supposed to be making me feel better?"

He gives his sad clown smile. "If you ever want to talk about it, I'm here."

"No, thank you."

He loses the trace of a smile. "You're a strong girl, honey. Really strong. In fact, I think you can handle just about anything."

I am thinking, You do not know me very well, then, Sam. I am no George Fox. If I were not already turned off religion, this would certainly do it for me.

"Don't you want to talk about what happened today?"

Jessica is behind him, holding a cup with steam rising from it. "Matt, I made you some tea." She squeezes past Sam and I smell the raspberry even before she gives me the mug.

"Thanks," I mumble. My hands are warm and the steam rises to my face, letting me hide. And that is where I want to be right now. Hidden.

Somehow Jessica knows this because she kisses the top of my head and walks quietly out of the room, tugging Sam's arm so he follows behind her. He is saying, "No, honey, I think—shouldn't we—" but Jessica shushes him.

She pops her head back in my room. "Matt, you know we're here for you whenever you want us, right?"

I nod, the mug in front of me, and she disappears, smiling, behind the steam.

CHAPTER TWENTY

That night I am freezing. It is so darn cold. Is it always this cold? Maybe I just never noticed.

I put my hand by the floor vent. There is only cold air blowing out. Why do we need air-conditioning when it is zero degrees outside?

I cannot sleep. I put on my jacket for the arctic walk to the thermostat downstairs. I flip on the switch in the half bath, leaving the door almost closed so the light does not wake up Sam and Jessica. There is enough light for me to read the thermostat, though. It is fifty-four degrees. Fifty-four is an outside temperature. What is an outside temperature doing inside?

I turn the dial up to eighty and think about Hawaii. I am waiting for the instant surge of sunshine. It does not come. Now I wish I had put my boots on because my feet, even in socks, are freezing. There is arctic air blasting them from the vent. I stamp them to keep them from turning to solid ice.

I hear a click and am blinded by light from the living room. There is a rustling, and Jessica comes out in her flannel nightgown and sweater. "Matt, honey, are you okay?"

"I am freezing."

She pushes the hair out of her face and looks at the thermostat.

"It does not work," I inform her. "It is not a real thermostat. It is a placebo-stat. It is only there to make you think you have control over the heat."

She shakes her head and grimaces. "It's the heat pump. It never feels warm. I hate it."

It is nice to hear Jessica hate something. No one should be all-loving. It is not normal.

She opens the hall closet and pulls at boxes on the top shelf. "Ah, here it is." She takes out a black and gray blanket-type thing and smiles at it. "This was my grandmother's shawl."

"The grandmother of the blue-dented-pot fame?"

Jessica laughs and shakes out the shawl. "One and the same. It's an angora wool shawl, which her mother, my great-grandmother, brought over from Ireland. There's a little rip somewhere. . . ." She examines the corners. "Ah, here it is." She holds up a corner with dark blue yarn woven through it. "I fixed it, thinking the blue would blend in enough." She scrunches her nose up. "Maybe if I were a better seamstress it would have, but I'm afraid sewing isn't my forte."

"It looks fine," I tell her. "I like the tassels." There are wispy, ghostly threads of yarn fringing the entire shawl. They start solid next to the body of the shawl and stretch out into such fine threads they seem to disappear into the air. There is something unearthly about them, as if they are tying together what is and what was.

Jessica smiles. "And it's warm and soft. Feel it."

I pull back. "I do not like wool. It makes me itch."

"Not this kind. This is as soft as cotton balls but so warm." She puts her face against it as if to prove her point.

I hesitate, then stroke the shawl like it is a cat. Jessica wraps it around my hand and I notice instant warmth. I let out a sigh.

"I want you to have this."

"For tonight?"

She smiles. "Forever."

"You will not miss it?"

She looks at me, still smiling. "Oh, I'll see it all the time, and I'll enjoy seeing you using it." She puts it around me, even over my head. "You remind me of my grandmother."

"That is because I look like a little old Irish peasant at the moment."

"No, I mean your personalities." Jessica puts her arm around the shawl, my jacket, and me, and gives a squeeze.

"She was somewhat obnoxious, I take it."

"No," Jessica says, giving a soft laugh and holding me close. "I loved her very, very much."

I do not know what to say. And I do not know why my nose is getting stuffy and I have to swallow so hard.

She strokes my shawl-head for a long time. It makes me warm and drowsy.

Finally, I yawn. "What was Grandmother-of-the-Shawl's name?"

"Maggie Mahone. She was full of wonderful stories, so I'm sure you'll have pleasant dreams." Jessica turns the bathroom light off and steers me toward the stairs, with a little hug. "Good night, Matt."

"Night." I pull the shawl tighter around me. It is cozy. "Thanks," I mumble. I am not sure if I am thanking Maggie Mahone or Jessica. I do not think Jessica heard me. Perhaps Maggie Mahone did.

take Maggie Mahone's shawl on the bus with me. It covers both me and my backpack. Still, I shrink in my seat.

The bus has to detour around some construction on lovely Route 229. We drive past the Meeting House, and I see what I had not seen when we left the day before. There is red paint, like splattered blood, all over the front of the Meeting House. I shudder. People—I recognize most of them, like Chuck and Laurie—are painting white over the blood. So far, you can still see the red oozing through.

The Rat and his Vermin crowd to my side of the bus to get a better view. I shrink down into my seat. They are jeering and snickering at the "whitewashers."

I pull Maggie Mahone's shawl tighter around me.

At lunchtime, the peace club is spilling out of the library conference room onto not one, but two large tables. I sit by myself at the third.

"Okay, everyone," Mrs. Jimenez says, trying to get everyone's attention. The librarian glares at her. "It's great to see so many of you," her voice strains a loud whisper, "but from now on our meetings will be immediately after school on Tuesdays. I'm afraid—well, glad—that we're getting to be such a large group we can't fit in a conference room, and we really can't hold meetings during the day in the library."

"Aw, man," a boy with long blond hair says, "I've got cross-country on Tuesdays starting next week."

"We're lucky we get to meet at all." I recognize one of the original students from several weeks ago. "If it were up to—uh, a certain teacher, we'd be banned."

"Let me guess," says a boy with a peace symbol on his shirt. "Does his last name start with *M*?"

I am thrown for a second because I was expecting to hear "*W*." Then I remember it is only me who calls him Mr. Warhead.

"Yeah, Rob, and he'd really like what you've done to your jeans!" someone says.

The peace shirt boy stands up, grinning, and I see his torn jeans and wonder what the big deal is. He turns his back to the tables and lifts his T-shirt but I cannot see his jeans because of all the people.

"So?" someone says. "It's an American flag."

"Dude!" someone yells back. "It's upside down! That's the symbol of distress."

Mrs. Jimenez smiles but shakes her head. "Please don't let . . . You Know Who see that."

"Voldemort?" Rob asks.

I am starting to like this Rob.

His large brown eyes are open wide but there is the slightest hint of a smile on his lips. He reminds me of an actor. I know! He looks like a younger version of Will Smith.

Mrs. Jimenez sighs. "Let's try to be understanding."

"Understanding?" Rob says. "What about the attack on that Quaker church—while people were inside?"

Mrs. Jimenez shudders. "Horrifying, I know. It's getting dangerous out there. You heard what the mayor said?"

"About the churches?" It is Susan. She shakes her head. "That'll never happen. I mean, some people might stop going to church, but churches—or synagogues either for that matter—aren't just going to close down for a few weeks."

"And why should they?" Rob asks. "What about freedom of religion? Freedom of assembly? Freedom of speech?"

"I know," Mrs. Jimenez says, "but the mayor has to keep his citizens safe. This is a small town with a lot of churches and temples, and he can't promise that every church will be surrounded by police since most of them have services at roughly the same time. There's only one peace vigil—Thursday nights—so he can cover that."

"But he still warned about the danger of going," Susan says quietly.

Rob kicks his feet off of a wooden chair so suddenly, the chair clatters to the floor.

"Shhhhh!" the librarian sputters.

Rob puts the chair upright but his teeth are clenched. He shakes his head. "Does anyone else feel like we're living in a totalitarian society? Supposedly, we're fighting to bring freedom and democracy to the rest of the world. Meanwhile, what's happening to freedom and democracy at home?"

There is no answer.

Rob looks around the room. "Why are we all just sitting here? Why don't we go see the mayor and tell him how we feel?"

"Right now?" someone asks.

"I don't mean cut class, I mean we should make an appointment and go tell him that this sucks." Rob's eyes flit from face to face, including mine. His eyes linger on mine and it is not scary but my heart does start beating faster.

"That's it!" He turns from me to Mrs. Jimenez. "Why don't we tell the mayor he should be stopping the local terrorists instead of telling innocent people to stop living their normal lives?"

The room rumbles with agreement and I am surprised to hear a "yes" escape from even my mouth before the librarian comes over and shushes us all.

At the end of the day, the bus leaves school using the detour and drives past the Meeting House again. I close my eyes. I cannot look. I let the shawl cover my ears so I cannot hear what the Rat says. I hear him laughing but I keep my head down and refuse to let him in.

My head is still down, in disappearing mode, when I step into Casa Quaker. Jessica is on the phone. She tugs on my shoulder and hands me a postcard of the interior of a church in Washington, D.C.

It is from Loopy. I wave to Jessica and walk upstairs, reading it.

> Hi, Matt!
>
> Hope you're settling in nicely. Got my work cut out for me here. Can you believe all these church attacks? The beautiful windows in this church are now broken. Be careful—it's happening all over!
>
> Love in Christ,
> Bernice (aka "Loopy")

I flip the card over and look at the red stained-glass windows and wonder how the inside of the church looked with shards of red glass.

I sigh and hear Jessica still talking on the phone.

"I know. I wish he wouldn't put himself in such danger. . . . Yes, I've tried to talk to him, but you know Sam. . . . My heart is in my throat every time he leaves the house."

I close my door. I do not want to hear this.

"Matt!" Jessica calls up the stairs.

I jump. "Yes."

"Honey, I have to run to the legal aid clinic. Sam will be home soon. Will you be all right by yourself?"

"I guess."

"Okay, see you later." I hear the front door open.

I open my door. "Wait!"

"Yes?"

"Where is . . . the kid?"

There is a pause. "*Rory* is at physical therapy. I'm picking him up on my way back."

"Oh."

"Are you going to be okay?"

"I will be fine."

"See you, sweetheart."

The front door closes.

It is the first time I have been in this house alone. It is strange. I do not like it. I go down to the kitchen, looking for signs of life. The computer is on and I walk over to it. I sit down on the wheely stool and look at the opened site.

CNN. BREAKING NEWS. A peace demonstration. In Washington, D.C. With pro-war activists. It spiraled out of control. Many are injured. One man is dead. I shudder when I read his name. Sam Hobbs. *Sam.*

It is just a name. And it was in Washington. But it was a peace demonstration. And it could happen anywhere. Like Loopy said, *Be careful—it's happening all over!*

I read the full version of the article. It lists the attacks around the country on churches, nonprofits, peace centers— any group that is trying to bring peace to this country, and all countries. There is much damage. And fear.

I am suddenly freezing cold, shivering, shaking. I run upstairs to put on my shawl. It does not seem to help. I grab my backpack and struggle with the zipper to get out my LifeSavers. Even with them, I do not like being upstairs by myself in this cold, dark house. I run downstairs and flick on every light I can find. I pace. I put my shawl over my head.

And I am still pacing. Up and down the steps now. Not happy in any place. At least I am a moving target.

I am making my turn at the bottom of the stairs to go back up when Sam comes in the front door. I jump.

"Hi, Matt, honey. Where's Jessica?"

"She is at the legal aid clinic, for God's sake!"

He slowly closes the door behind him. "Are you okay, Matt?"

"I am fine!" I turn and go into the kitchen, then remember that I cannot go in there because of the BREAKING NEWS, and I step out again. "Have you people never heard of screen savers?"

I go upstairs to my room and sit down on the bed. I am clutching my LifeSavers in my fist.

My door is open a little so I hear Sam when he groans and hits some keys on the keyboard. Then I hear him come up the steps. They creak and sigh under his great weight.

He is standing outside my door. "Hi. It's me again. Looks like I'm becoming a regular here at Matt's Place." He smiles. Obviously, he is trying to be witty. It is not a Quaker talent.

I stare at him through the crack. I do not smile.

He sighs and gently pushes my door open. "Look, honey, the police will offer some protection next First Day so we can all feel secure at worship."

I stare at him. "You mean, so *you* can feel secure at worship—falsely secure, I might add. I, myself, am never going anywhere near that Meeting House again."

Sam's eyes look like I have kicked him. "I guess I can't blame you. But, if you change your mind—"

"I will not change my mind." What kind of idiot do you think I am, Sam?

He sits down on the bed next to me and it sinks almost to the floor. I struggle to keep myself from falling sideways into him.

I can hear his breathing and his warm breath comes out softly and steadily. "I was just going to say, I'll always be there to protect you, Matt."

"And what if they come with guns next time, Sam? How will you protect me from that?"

He shakes his head. "I don't think that would happen. I think they're just kids. Or people who are frustrated, upset."

"I think they are just crazy. You cannot predict what crazy people will do, Sam." My voice is rising and I can feel the tornado swirling inside of me again. I wonder why the tornado is there when I know that I can avoid the danger. I will simply never go back. I look at Sam and I realize why I am quaking. He is actually planning to be a Sitting Duck of Death on Sunday. "You would stay away from that place, too, if you had any brains."

His eyes grow wide and his mouth drops open. "The Meeting House? I could never stay away from there. It's part of my life."

"It could be part of your death."

"Matt—" He lays his hand on my arm but my arm convulses so much I throw his hand off.

He folds his hands together in his lap and looks down. His eyes are closed. I am not sure if he is thinking or praying. Or waiting for God's Voice to tell him what to do.

I stare at him. His MIA bracelet is sticking out from under the sleeve of his sweatshirt. Which has gack on it, from the kid, no doubt. The front of his sweatshirt says "Peace Takes Guts." There are six photos of people under the slogan. The Sweatshirt People of Peace, who are probably all dead, grow larger and smaller, along with Sam's belly as he breathes. Then the sweatshirt people twist toward me and I look up at Sam's face.

He is smiling. "You sound like Jessica. She's worried, too."

I exhale loudly. "Because she is not an idiot. It is two against one, and you, Sam, are outvoted."

He grins. "But I have God on my side."

"Oh, please!"

He presses his lips together and the grin goes away. His eyes are boring through me. "If I stay away, if we close the Meeting House, who wins?"

I look away.

"I won't let that happen, Matt. You understand that, I know, because you wouldn't, either."

I flash my eyes at him.

"I mean, if you felt as I do about this issue, you wouldn't give in. You're too strong for that. You wouldn't let them win."

I think about my battle with Mr. Warhead and how I will

not give in. But that is different. I do not expect Mr. Warhead to come to class with a gun and shoot me. If that were a possibility, I would not fight him. I would run away. And I thought Quakers did the same thing. "Sam. You are a Quaker. You are not supposed to fight."

"Who said anything about fighting? I'm just standing my ground."

"Could you find a safer piece of ground upon which to stand?"

He shrugs. "I can't hide. I can't run away from the things I want to change."

"Why not? It is a strategy that has always worked for me."

He looks at me with eyes that are both sad and serious. "I want peace, Matt. I want people to resolve conflicts without resorting to war, to killing."

"That is very nice, Sam, but just because you are a Quaker does not mean you have the monopoly on peace."

The Sweatshirt People of Peace jolt. "Of course not. I—I never said that. Peace isn't even a religious issue. It's individuals, and groups, like the Resource Center for Nonviolence that I work with, all the way up to the UN. I just happen to be Quaker and believe—"

"Okay, there are many peace organizations in this world, Sam. Why not let the professionals handle it?"

"I—I am. I'm in touch with the Lombard Peace Center, too—they're a Mennonite group—"

"Has anyone attacked the Mennonite Meeting House?"

"Church. And, no, not that I'm aware of."

"So why not go to the Mennonite Church? I mean, how different could you people be, really? You all believe in God, right? Who cares about the details?"

"But I'm a Quaker!"

I stare at him like he is an Ignorant Child. "Okay." I exhale loudly. "What do you have to believe if you are a Quaker? Because I am sure the Mennonites will not mind."

"I don't *have* to believe anything." He smiles. "That's what I like about my faith."

"You are very exasperating."

He gives me a wink. "See, there you go again, acting like Jessica. In fact, it almost sounds like you care about me."

I roll my eyes, cross my arms, and turn away. "Remember to close the door on your way out, thank you."

"No," he says, getting up, "thank *you*."

I look at him involuntarily. He is standing with his gack-covered arm on the doorknob. His eyes are puppylike under his tousled hair. He is smiling a shy smile at me. I look away. When I look back, he is gone. I stare at the place he stood.

I am squeezing my LifeSavers so hard, I think the foil is cutting into me.

CHAPTER TWENTY-TWO

At the end of the day, I am at my locker and I smell it. Beer, again. The Rat, again. And I see the Wall. I shut my locker and quickly walk away from the Wall.

But I do not want to ride the bus. I turn down a corridor to think. I decide to walk to Casa Quaker. It is probably a couple of miles, maybe less. The only reason we have a bus is that Route 229 is too narrow and dangerous to make us walk. But today I want to. I cannot handle seeing the Meeting House again. I also would rather avoid certain passengers on the bus.

It is a nice change not to have to rush to the parking lot, so I relish the slow pace and take my time walking through the halls. I look around the school, seeing it, in a way, for the first time. Normally I do not look up, so I am very familiar with the floor, but nothing else. And it is usually too crowded to see the walls, anyway, because I am in so much of a hurry to get to class without being noticed that I never look.

There is actually much on the walls. Notices about senior class picture retakes and senior class rings. A sign for the drama department's production of *West Side Story*. Posters for Odyssey of the Mind, chess club, cheerleading practice, and my favorite, one on antibullying.

It is mostly quiet as I wander the hallways. I like school much better this way. No people, or very few, at least. The teachers and handful of students ignore me. They have important things to do, and they assume I do, too.

I saunter down the hall and the south stairwell toward the front door. Instead of scurrying down the stairs with my head tucked in, I take each step slowly, with my head held high. I am in a fashion show, today sporting a lovely designer Maggie Mahone wool wraparound skirt over my pants. The style is black on black, with black accessories. My hair is enviously big. It has been said that I have beautiful skin and haunting eyes. I pause, giving my imaginary fans a chance to take it all in. It is an elegant look. Occasionally, I nod to the adoring crowd.

I hear real crowd noises coming from a classroom. It is a double-wide classroom, the dividing curtain opened to make a huge room. There is much talking and laughing. I walk toward the open door and see Rob writing "Peace Ideas" on the whiteboard.

The peace club has found a new home. I look around the hallway. They have guts to hold this club in the shadow of the American flag hanging over Principal Patterson's Patriotic Office. And the posters for the Army, Air Force, Navy, and Marines surrounding the guidance counselor's broom closet down the hall.

I hover in the doorway, watching Rob draw a peace sign next to his heading on the whiteboard. I actually have some ideas for the peace club. They could bring in speakers to give the other side of the war story. They could set up a debate between Mr. Warhead and someone who is actually sane. That I would like to see. They could put out a newsletter about what is really happening in the "Middle Eastern Theater" because, the truth is, most students are ignorant of world events in general. I bet most would not even know where those countries are, for God's sake. Until recently, most people would probably have thought that Islam was one of the many "I" countries. There could be articles on what life is like in those other cultures so people could begin to understand them and realize that they are not like us and that, in some ways, not being like us is not such a bad thing. There should be a list of websites so that people could go check for themselves if they do not believe what is in the newsletter. It would be easy. They are already bookmarked on Sam's computer.

I notice Mrs. Jimenez at a desk in the front of the room talking with a group of kids. She is laughing. Now she is leaning back in a chair, stretching her arms behind her head and flipping her long black hair. It is gorgeous. She does not look very teacherlike. Several students are joking with her, including Rob, as if they are equals. They are all slapping each other on the back, even slapping Mrs. Jimenez's back. She does not look like she is going to give them a detention, either.

It is like watching a sitcom on TV. Everyone is laughing and happy. I always wonder if real people can have sitcom lives. Apparently, it is possible. My life is the serious docudrama. Or horror flick.

And then I hear the snort of the Rat behind me. My chest tightens. I whip around so as not to be attacked from behind.

He is coming out of the principal's office.

I am a lone target in the hallway.

"You!" he hisses.

I want to run. Or hide. Step into the peace room. Maybe there are enough people there to stand up to the Rat. Maybe.

But I cannot even turn away. My legs are wobbling and my hands, no, my entire arms are shaking. I can hear my heavy breathing.

He is speaking at me but his Rat face and his Rat words are swimming before my eyes. *Do not look into his eyes.* I am cowering, trying to get away from his Rat eyes.

"I know you're the one who told Patterson!"

I do not even know what he is talking about.

"Don't look so innocent. You told him about the booze!"

Now I remember the Rat and his friends drinking at his locker. I shake my head and finally break the tractor beam and I can look away.

"Well, girl, you're dead."

"Richard! What are you doing?"

I recognize Principal Patterson's voice from the morning announcements and realize I have never seen him in person before.

The Rat whips around.

"The late bus is that way." Patterson points his long bony finger down the hall.

The Rat swaggers off, but not before he stares at me with his black eyes, and mouths the words again: "You're dead."

I am quaking so much I think I will either explode or

implode, I am not sure which. This is it. I am dead. The Rat's gray lips tell me, over and over, that I am dead.

"And what are you doing here, young lady?" It is Principal Patterson's voice again.

I jump. I do not have an answer. I simply stare at his ill-fitting navy blazer and clashing brown shirt. And I see the Rat disappear around the corner to the left at the end of the hall.

"Are you here for a particular activity?"

Slowly, I shake my head.

He looks me up and down, squeezing his lips together, perhaps noticing my dark fashion statement. "Well, there's no loitering after school. Go on home!" He turns around and disappears into the office.

I walk shakily down the hall, casting a last glance at the peace room. I pull my shawl around me. The hall is now empty, almost eerie, and my footsteps make too much noise. I move slowly, barely inching along, hoping the Rat has already made it to the buses. At least I will be turning right at the end of the hall, away from the Rat.

I speed up to pass the military posters and my guidance counselor's closet and get to my corner because now I sense an urgency to get out of here. I need to turn the corner fast.

That is when the Rat leaps out in front of me—from *my* corner—and a scream sticks in my throat and blocks my airway so I cannot even breathe.

"I'll get you," he hisses, directly at me. He puts his fingers around his neck and jerks it to one side, making a choking sound. "Sometime, somewhere, when you're not looking, I'll get you." He drops his hands from his neck and lunges at me and I stumble back and turn and run and I can hear him behind me, his snide laughter and his boots, but they are getting farther away. He is not following me. I stop, panting, and listen to his boots pounding down the steps. On the stairwell that he snuck down, then up, so he could jump out and scare me.

I stand there for a long time, not knowing where I can go to be safe. The voices from the peace room drift into my head and catch me. I want to turn and follow them but it is too dangerous. What if the Rat sees me going into the peace room? It will only make things worse.

I go to the opposite end of the building and hide in the shadow of the north stairwell, quaking, until I hear the late buses leaving. I strain to look out the window to see if the Rat is on any of them. I wait for a while, scanning the parking lot and the playing fields, wanting to be certain that the Rat is not waiting to pounce on me.

Finally, I take Maggie Mahone's shawl from my waist and put it over my head. I am hoping the Spirit of Maggie Mahone will protect me. I am hoping she can make me invisible. I leave the school building and the door slams behind me. I shudder, as my eyes dart around the parking lot. It appears to be empty.

I think about the Rat's threat and how painful it is. I remember that pain. It has been a long time now, but I remember. It was after he ripped me from my mother's arm and threw her aside. He pulled my arms behind me so hard that I heard them pop and when he finally let go, they hung awkwardly at my sides and I thought they would not work again. But I forgot that pain when his arm came around my neck and I was choking and could not breathe and like a snake his grip became tighter every time I tried to yell until there was no air at all and I passed out.

A truck roars past and blasts its horn at me, nearly knocking me into the highway. When I turn off the main road, I am still shaking. It is almost dark and the lights are on at Casa Quaker. And Jessica is outside, without a coat, holding the phone in one hand, looking up the street.

CHAPTER TWENTY-THREE

Jessica comes running and grabs me. "Matt, are you all right?"

"I am fine," I lie, but I cannot seem to make my voice sound strong. Soon I will be dead. That is what the Rat said.

"What happened? Did something go wrong at school?" She is bending down, looking at my face, trying to see inside me.

"I—I just missed the bus."

"Oh, honey! If that ever happens again, please call me. I'll come get you if I have the car; otherwise, I'll get hold of Sam and he can come get you, okay?" She is peering into my eyes, clutching me.

I have to look away. I cannot answer. My throat hurts too much.

Jessica puts her arms around me and gives me a long hug. I do not hug her back. I do not know how. But now I notice the cold air. It is stinging my eyes.

"Come on, let's go inside. I'll make some hot chocolate to warm you up."

But she still does not let go. She keeps hugging me, squeezing me, like she will be there forever.

My throat is dry, but the lump in my throat is so large that I cannot even swallow.

Stop, I say to myself, hoping Jessica will hear. Please do not be so nice to me when I am already down, Jessica. It is too much for me to handle. I am too weak to fight. My armor is only so strong.

She walks me inside and makes me take my backpack off. I let the heavy, cumbersome weight slide to the floor and I am lighter. I sit at the table and Jessica puts a mug of hot chocolate in front of me, with miniature marshmallows in it. It smells hot and creamy and comforting and encouraging. Jessica's mug of raspberry tea is next to me, and the fruity scent is blending with the chocolate into something soft and kind. My hands are thawing around my hot mug.

My whole body is thawing in the warmth of the kitchen and the sound of Jessica's voice as she stands at the stove chattering away about how the kid has grown an inch and Phyllis from Meeting has joined the Library Committee, which will be so good for her, and how much Sam is enjoying being a bus driver because the younger kids are so cute and the older kids need someone to talk to and Sam is such a good listener.

The kid is making his sounds like "awsh," and "Saaa," and "Maaa," as well as banging his blue pot on the floor. Strangely, the noise does not bother me. The light, the sound, the steam from the pot on the stove are all insulating layers, like Maggie Mahone's shawl.

Jessica sets a cutting board, knife, and some peeled potatoes in front of me. "Little pieces, for the soup," she says.

Still I cannot speak. I just nod and do what she says.

Jessica keeps chattering away, occasionally patting my back or squeezing my shoulder or stroking my hair.

Now I am chopping celery. I do not even like celery but the smell does not bother me.

Sam comes in with a "how's my girl?" I think he is talking to Jessica. By the time I realize he is talking to me, he is walking over to Jessica to give her a kiss. Then he picks up the kid.

"Saaa, Saaa," the kid gurgles. "Saaa-uh-Saaa, Saaa-uh-Saaa!"

Sam and Jessica laugh and cuddle with the kid. They turn to look at me, to see if I understand. I nod my head. I know that the kid is saying "Sam-I-Am" from hearing Sam read *Green Eggs and Ham* a thousand times. Jessica gives me a hug and Sam winks at me, as if I am part of it. I suppose I am, in a way, because we are the only three people in the world who could possibly know what the kid is saying.

We are sitting in the warm, tingly, steamy kitchen with soup bowls in front of us. The kid is now singing, sort of, and Sam and Jessica are laughing. There is laughter and chatter all around me. It is like no kitchen I have ever known.

I am looking at my soup. I love this soup. I want to hide in this soup, among its carrots and potatoes and celery and chicken and warm breath. I could read myself to sleep with the words I would string together out of all the tiny alphabet noodles. I want to fall asleep in this soup, wrapping myself in its wide noodles and using a soft lima bean for a pillow.

The kid puts his chubby little hand gently on mine, then squeezes my hand several times, with a cooing sound. His hand is warm and sticky but for some reason I do not mind. Usually I cannot stand someone sticking to me.

"That's the first time I've seen that," Jessica says softly, as Sam's hand moves on top of hers.

I know that the kid sees Sam and Jessica do it all the time.

I stare into the soup and imagine I am in its warmth.

Then I hear Jessica's voice, soft, coming through the soup. "I think our Matt had a rough day."

Jessica leans her head toward me. Her hair is touching my hair. Now the solid firmness of her head is against my head. It is somewhat odd but not unpleasant. I decide that it is all right to relax my neck a little and let my head rest against hers. Her head is already there, anyway. So it hardly counts.

CHAPTER TWENTY-FOUR

I t is breakfast. Jessica forces me to eat now. We have an agreement. I will eat one piece of not-too-burnt toast. With the good kind of raspberry jam. Seedless. Black raspberry, not red. And she and Sam must keep their coffee mugs on the other side of the table so I am not predisposed to puke.

But this morning I feel like puking and it is not the coffee's fault.

Sam sits down at the table with a grin. "Guess what! I get to be the sub on your bus starting tomorrow, Matt!"

I drop my toast. "What? Why?"

"Because Wanda had her baby last night."

I pick up my napkin. "Who is Wanda?"

"Your bus driver."

I start shredding my napkin. "My bus driver?"

"Yes. Didn't you even know her name?"

In truth, I did not even know she was a woman. She was a nameless, faceless, shapeless mass that propelled the Bus from Hell. That is all.

"She had a little girl," Sam says, as if I am interested.

"Oh, that's wonderful!" croons Jessica.

It is not wonderful. I am thinking of the implications.

"There must be other substitute drivers, Sam. Surely one of them can take my route."

"Don't you want me to drive your bus?"

"It is not a good group of kids, Sam." I say it partly to put him off because no, I do not want him driving my bus. For my own self-preservation, I cannot be associated with Sam the Quaker. Also, I say it for his own good because I think the Rat will make scrapple out of the grinning Incredible Quaker Hulk. "You may want to choose another route."

He smiles and shrugs his shoulders up, holding them there a moment. "I thought it'd be kind of fun for us to be together." He looks, as usual, like a happy, oversized child.

He really does not get it.

Jessica's eyes are searching my face and she puts her hand on mine.

I sigh. I know what she is telling me. Do not be mean to him. He cares. "Fine, Sam. Do not say I did not warn you."

Jessica smiles at me.

Sam smiles even more and takes a large bite of scrapple.

I cannot eat a thing. To be honest, part of me is relieved that Sam will be on the bus because I do not believe Sam will let the Rat murder me. However, I am wondering how a Quaker can prevent a murder without using violence, since violence is entirely un-Quakerish. So I am not entirely comfortable. And I really do not want Sam to blow my cover. If he starts spouting his Quaker-speak, and I am identified as being associated with him, then the Rat will make scrapple out of both of us. My lap is covered with shredded napkin.

The phone rings and I jump. Sam and Jessica look at

each other. Jessica pushes back from the table but Sam's chair is closer and he only has to stand up and reach to grab the receiver from the wall.

"Hello?" His forehead is wrinkled. "Oh, good morning, Jake."

Jessica is staring at him but his face reveals nothing.

"Uh-huh . . . okay . . . anything else?" He nods. "Okeydoke! I'll see you shortly. Bye." He hangs up, sits down, and starts to take another bite of scrapple.

Jessica gives an exasperated cry. "Well?"

Sam looks up with the innocent face that he does so badly. "What?"

Jessica narrows her eyes. "You know what I mean."

He sighs and puts his fork down. "Someone called the Meeting House this morning. And about half a dozen other houses of worship. Probably kids. Just a prank, I'm sure."

Jessica's voice is hard and her eyes are boring into Sam. "What did they say?"

"Just something about watching ourselves."

Jessica's voice is shrieky. "I knew it! They're going to attack again!"

The kid wails a chilling scream that stops her.

Sam shakes his head fast. "Not now, honey. Rory." She stands up and turns away from the table, her shoulders dropping and her hands covering her face.

Sam stands and picks up the kid. "Jake called the police and they'll be at Meeting this morning, so nothing's going to happen." He huddles the kid against his chest with one arm and reaches for Jessica with his other, pulling her into his chest, too, and resting his cheek on the top of her head.

"It's okay, baby, it's okay," he says, and I do not know which one of them he is speaking to.

Suddenly it does not matter that Sam will be a bus driver on my bus. What matters is that he may never make it to the bus. It is First Day today. I hope it is not his Last Day. The rest of us are staying home.

I cannot look when Sam leaves. I hear Sam and Jessica saying good-bye. They are using their love words, like *honey* and *sweetheart*. I do not begrudge them those words today. This may be their Last Chance. The door closes and I bite my lip, harder when the kid calls out, "Saaa-uh-Saaaaa!" I listen to the noisy Subaru pull out and I wish it would break down before it even reaches the main road.

I mumble something about homework and run upstairs to my room, shutting the door, trying to shut out the kid. Sitting on the bed, I stare at my knickknack thingy. It looks small and weak. Still, I check to see if the LifeSaver is inside. It is, but for some reason the *swoosh-crunch* of the lid is not comforting me. I pull *A Beautiful Mind* from the bookshelf but no matter how hard I try, I cannot focus on it. It could be because of the moans from the kid. I try another book, *Nathan's Run*. It is all about a scared boy who is alone, being hunted down even though he is innocent. I know I should put it back but somehow I am pulled into the story and stay there until a particularly loud wail from the kid jerks me free. I am panting, like the boy in the book. I have gotten far enough to know that Nathan cannot run forever and is going to have to trust someone. I run downstairs to the kitchen.

Jessica walks in, holding the kid, rubbing her head. It is

another migraine day for her. I grab the huge aspirin bottle from the cupboard and slam it down on the counter, harder than I mean to. Jessica jumps. To make up for it, I pour her a glass of water and rest it gently on the counter, spilling only a little. I wrestle with the cap of the bottle and get two aspirins out and hand them to her.

She smiles. "How did you know?"

"Your eyes."

I grab *Green Eggs and Ham* from the counter and start to read. It does not stop the kid from moaning. I am not Sam. He sits on the floor, his head hanging down, not even touching the blue pot that lies next to him. I read loud and fast, sounding like one of those drug commercials that has to squeeze in the twenty-nine horrible side effects you may suffer just to keep your nose from running.

I am done with the book and the kid is still moaning. Jessica picks him up and kisses the top of his head. She walks over to the computer keyboard and presses a key. The CNN homepage appears. I hear her moan and click the mouse. A video begins about more horrors in the Middle East.

I remember watching CNN from my childhood. I have always had this fantasy that I am Christiane Amanpour, the reporter who is in the middle of every horrible event. It is a fantasy because I do not ever want to be where she is, either in a war zone or in front of the camera. I just want the whole world to know the stories. Even if the stories are painful. Otherwise, those people, important people, will be forgotten. You will not even be able to conjure up an image of her face, no matter how hard you try. All you will remember are the ambulances and police cars. And the sirens. Always the sirens. Screaming. Wailing. And, finally, dying.

I realize that I am reading the BREAKING NEWS at the top of the screen, looking to see if a Quaker Meeting House has just been bombed. I look away and see Jessica staring hard at the monitor, her face taut and pinched, eyes squeezed, like she is examining every pixel, waiting for them to explode.

She reminds me of my mother, who always watched CNN. She wanted to know what was going on, but she called it "nasty news." I remember that. It was always "nasty news." That is why, for the longest time, I thought CNN meant "*See* Nasty News."

She stood when the news was on. Like Jessica is now. I do not know if it was because the TV was in the kitchen and she was always cooking or if she could not take the news sitting down. I do remember that she watched every day and talked back to the TV. Sometimes she would try to reason with the reporter, in that motherly voice. Other times, she would actually yell at the TV person, one hand on her hip and the other shaking a finger at him. That scared me a little. Or she would stand there and cry, grabbing a napkin from the counter to wipe her eyes. Like Jessica is doing now. That was the worst. That was when I wanted to kick that smug newscaster, in his suit and tie, and say, "Shut up, dork!"

I look back at the monitor. The newscaster says that eleven more soldiers have been captured and tortured, their bodies dragged through the streets, before they were even dead. Jessica closes her eyes and moans. Like my mother. Like I did, too, at first just imitating her; then, because I felt her anguish; afterward, because I felt my own. Some news drives a knife into that feeling part of your brain that is directly connected to your stomach, causing nausea, and sending it into spasms that reverberate all the way back up to your brain and make you dizzy. I am shaking.

"Retaliation will be swift and severe," the newscaster promises. "U.S. troop strength will be increased to—"

"Shut up, dork!" I am standing, shouting at the monitor. "Shut *up*, dork!"

Jessica holds the kid close to her. They are both staring at me. Jessica grabs the mouse and clicks on the window, closing it down. "It's okay," she says softly.

"No, it is not okay!" I shout, and I yell some other things to the monitor, even though the newscaster is gone now. They are worse than "Shut up, dork," and Jessica asks me to please stop, that I need to watch my language so that the kid does not pick it up.

I take a deep breath and stop the shouting but the quaking continues. Jessica is still wiping her eyes with a napkin. I grab one, too. And start shredding.

Jessica's eyes dart toward the window and she gasps. I look outside and see it, too. A police car. I think we all stop breathing, even the kid. Jessica and I run to the door at the same time. We step out into the frigid air. Sam pulls up behind the police car. At first, I think the Subaru has been rammed. Then I remember it always looks like that. We run to the street.

Sam is getting out of the car and waving to the police car, which keeps on going.

"What was that all about?" Jessica asks, her voice breathy.

Sam shuts the car door and smiles. "Just giving me a police escort home."

"Why?" I ask, also breathy.

"To make me feel safe, I think. Isn't that nice? Going

above and beyond the call of duty." He gives Jessica a kiss and takes the kid from her.

Jessica and I look at each other. We know that a police escort is not normal. It is not something the police do just to be nice. I look back at Sam. He is so naïve. Or he is hiding something.

CHAPTER TWENTY-FIVE

The next day, I step onto the bus and see Sam smiling widely at me.

Oh, God. He has found his dork cap.

"Good morning, Matt!"

I stare at him.

He extends his right hand, for what, I do not know. "How's my—"

I hear the Rat guffawing from somewhere near the third row and rush past Sam, down the aisle, bury my head, throw myself into a seat, and cower.

I am dead. Dead, Sam!

I am still cringing when the door opens again at the next stop and I hear Sam's voice.

"Good morning, Susan! Good morning, Will! My name's Sam."

There is more laughter. The Rat guffaws again. And, slowly, I realize that Sam is not singling me out. Again, at the next stop, Sam greets people by name. How does he know everyone's name?

"Hi, I'm Sam. Which one of you is Zach and which is Peter?"

I hear some mumbled responses.

"Great, well, good morning, Pete! And good morning, Zach!"

I peep over the seat back in front of me. Pete and Zach, whichever is which, are looking stunned. The Rat is still laughing.

I watch as we slow down for the next stop. Sam runs his finger along a list on a clipboard hanging from a knob on the dash. It must be a list of who gets on at what stop. He opens the door.

"Good morning, Robert! Do you prefer Robert or Bob?"

Robert or Bob is standing stiffly on the top step. "Uh, it's Rob."

Peace Club Rob?

"Good morning, Rob!" Sam sticks his hand out and Rob shakes hands with him.

And I see it is Peace Club Rob. He sits down on the seat directly behind Sam. Why have I never noticed him on the bus before? Oh, probably because I never look at anyone on the Bus from Hell.

The Rat hoots. "Jeez, this guy must be on drugs. He thinks he's driving the Sesame Street bus!" The Rat starts singing, "Can you tell me how to get, how to get to Sesame Street?"

All of the Vermin laugh. And some nonvermin, too.

And I hope against hope that Sam will not start singing the George Fox song. *Please,* Sam, do not sing!

As if he is reading my mind, Sam looks in the rearview mirror and gives a grin.

But he does not start singing. Maybe there is a God, after all.

173

The Rat calls out, "I need to get me some of whatever this dude's taking! Someone get me drugs like his!"

Sam must hear, but he ignores it.

I am relieved when we pull into the school parking lot. Until Sam says "have a great day!" and "see you this afternoon!" and even—my stomach lurches—"learn lots!" as people leave the bus. Is he trying to make himself look like a fool, for God's sake? Some of the students laugh at him. Surprisingly, some actually say "bye" or "see ya." I am not one of them, in case the Rat sees. I do not even look at Sam. I am not proud of that but it is necessary. I hold my breath until I am off the bus and I can breathe again.

Until second period when Mr. Warhead asks me to stay after World Civ and shuts the classroom door. He walks back to the front of the classroom and I shrink down in my desk, block his view with my textbook, and start scribbling. I know I should not write on my desk in front of him, but I am so nervous I cannot stop myself.

"Your term paper." He presses his lips together hard.

Fatima?

"I am offended by it," he says.

I want to say, "I am offended by your hirsute nostrils, so we are even," but I do not.

"You are receiving an F." His voice is quiet and cool. He knows he is victorious.

I swallow and scribble harder.

"May I remind you, the term paper is worth sixty percent of your grade."

I am nauseous.

Mr. Warhead babbles on about extra-credit projects that may enable me to pass.

My scribbling finally takes on direction and meaning and my pen is making sweeping arches on the desktop and madly coloring in triangles and I am not even listening.

And then his fist hits my desk hard and I jump.

"How dare you?" His voice is ragged. "Now you get a detention, too, for defacing school property! Report to room 2B10 tomorrow afternoon!"

His angry spit lands on the giant peace symbol I made on my desk and I wonder, Who is doing the defacing now?

That afternoon, the Rat is not on the bus. I peer out the window as the bus idles in the parking lot. Then I see him. With the Wall. The Wall moves to the large dented sedan and gets inside. I wonder where the Rat and the Wall go and what they do. But I am glad he is not on the bus.

His Vermin are quiet without their ringleader. The rest of the bus is chatty. Rob is sitting in the front seat behind Sam again, talking to him. Sam is laughing. I am not sure that bus drivers are allowed to laugh. I am sure I have never heard one do that.

At Casa Quaker, Jessica is laughing. "Matt! Listen to Rory! It's amazing!" She clears her throat and looks at the kid. "O—kay?" she says slowly.

He looks up from the floor, grinning. "Tayyyy!" He starts clapping and so does she.

"See? He's saying okay!" Jessica looks at me. She is positively giddy.

I nod. It is not exactly "okay," but it is a big step for him.

When Sam arrives, he is just as thrilled as Jessica.

I decide not to ruin their excitement by telling them about my detention. I remember that the peace club meets on Tuesday afternoons, so I tell Sam I will not be on the bus tomorrow so I can stay for a meeting after school. It is not exactly a lie.

Sam's face lights up. "The peace club! Good for you, Matt! I'm so glad—"

"Wait. I did not say I am joining. I am just staying after school this one time." I pause, thinking of my stellar relationship with Mr. Warhead. "Although, I suppose it could happen again."

The next morning, I remind Sam that I will not be on the bus after school.

He beams as he gets ready to go. "Right! Peace club! You know, Rob's in that club. He's on our bus."

"Oh. Yes. Rob, the talker."

"Say hi to him for me at the meeting this afternoon, okay?"

I do not want to lie to Sam so I tell him the truth, as much as I can. "I will say hello to Rob."

When I am in the hall that day, I see Rob talking with some boys.

I stop in front of them. "Hello, Rob." I move on.

"Uh . . . good morning—yeah, uh, Matt." His voice is drowning out behind me but I nod my head in case he can see. I imagine he is still in shock.

Mr. Warhead assigns me an essay to write in detention: "Why I Am Fortunate to Be an American." I know he thinks I do not even deserve to be an American, that somehow I say the things I do because I hate my country. He would never believe that I actually care, that I do not want to see our soldiers or anyone else hurt, that I know what it is like to be hurt, that I know what it is like to have someone else invade your space and be all-powerful. Why does he refuse to listen to another opinion? Why does he refuse to see that in America we are allowed to give opinions? In fact, we are supposed to do this, for God's sake. That is the whole point.

I write down more than he probably wants to hear. I tell him that I am fortunate because I have freedom of religion, speech, and assembly. But also that I am free not to be religious, not to speak, and not to assemble. I can hate religion and refuse to worship anything and no one can hurt me. I can think that we are causing the world more problems by invading other countries and I will not be punished. And I can say we are invading them just because we want oil or a strategic position or the president is trying to score points, and no one can put me in prison for saying this. And everyone else is equally free to think that I am an idiot. But they cannot kill me or torture me. I can count on my freedoms with my very life because they include the most precious freedom of all: freedom from fear. I know my country will protect me because it cares about my freedoms—cares about *me*! This country unrelentingly follows fair and just rules. Unlike terrorists. Unlike bullies. Unlike the Rat.

After I finish, I stare out the windows of the detention hall and think how stupid I am to even try to make Mr. Warhead understand.

I hear purposeful feet coming down the corridor. Then I see Mrs. Jimenez walk by quickly. On her way to the peace club meeting, where I supposedly am right now. All of a sudden, the fast feet stop and Mrs. Jimenez's long black hair swings around the open door.

"Matt?" she mouths. Her eyes are in shock. Apparently, she is not used to her AP students being thrown in After-School Prison.

She walks into the quiet room, up to my desk. "What are you doing here?" she asks in a low voice.

I shrug. "Mr. Warhead does not like my political views."

She turns her head to one side, wrinkling her forehead.

"He does not like my peace stance."

"Oh, Mr. Morehead." Her face looks as if she has just popped an entire bag of Sour Skittles in her mouth. "I see." She stands there for several moments, moving her mouth and swallowing, trying to get rid of the taste.

Finally, she pats my hand and looks earnestly into my eyes. "We can change things." I look at her eyes and they are clear and bright like Sam's. Only they are not blue, like Sam's, but beautifully brown, to match her skin. I notice for the first time how Mrs. Jimenez glows. Perhaps she has an Inner Light. I am sure she would understand Fatima. Someday I might introduce her to Fatima. The three of us could probably cause quite a stir.

Mrs. Jimenez calls the prison warden teacher into the hallway.

I hear urgent whispers—Mrs. Jimenez. And bland mumblings—Warden Teacher. I cannot hear the conversation, even though I lean my whole body closer to the door.

I almost fall off my chair when Mrs. Jimenez's voice suddenly explodes. "Oh, that is just ridiculous! For heaven's—"

"Listen!" Warden Teacher is insistent and mumbling again.

Mrs. Jimenez answers and her voice is softer, quieter, but still firm. I miss some of the words. "I know that his son . . .

and died in Iraq . . . sorry, of course, but . . . over there in the first place—"

"Shhh!" And the conversation drops to a rumbling.

I am stunned. Now I know what happened to Mr. Warhead. He is a Victim, like his son. God. How awful. And I feel bad for him. So I add something at the bottom of my paper. "Sorry. I did not know about your son. I am really, really, really sorry."

But my sympathy is short-lived. The next day Mr. Warhead shakes the paper in my face. It has a red circle around my comment at the bottom but the words he hisses himself: "Don't think you can use cheap tricks to get a better grade out of me!"

I wonder if he even read my essay.

I press my fingers into the peace symbol gouged out of my desk. Like Mrs. Jimenez, I am sorry that his son was killed. I do not want anyone's son or daughter killed. But that is no excuse to turn abusive yourself. I suppose he is going to fail me. I guess I should be grateful that he is not allowed to hurt me any more than that.

When I look up, the Rat is staring at me. He clutches his arm with the other hand and does a sharp twist, uttering a sickening *crrreak* sound out of his leering mouth, and I look away fast.

CHAPTER TWENTY-SIX

G ood morning, shit-head!" the Rat calls to the girl getting on the bus.

"Good morning, shit-for-brains!" he yells to the boy behind her, and then he cracks up. The Rat is laughing at his own brilliance, as usual.

At the next stop, "Good morning, you piece of shit!"

More laughter from the Rat and his gang, but none from anyone else. The air is positively charged. It is as if an electrical storm could start at any moment.

Sam pulls the bus over to the side of the road and stops.

The laughing stops, too. Except for the Rat's.

Sam puts on the parking brake and turns off the engine. And waits.

Outside, traffic is roaring by, rain is falling, and it is dark gray. Inside, it is still, silent, and bright. Even the fluorescent bus lights are shining full force. Sam must have changed the bulbs.

The Rat is quiet in the motionless bus. For a minute or two. Then he starts laughing again, punches one of his Vermin, and looks like he is about to say something.

Sam stands up and turns in one movement. The bus lurches.

That stops the Rat.

Sam is a very large man.

Sam starts walking down the aisle. Heavily. It is the only way he can move. It is an accident of girth.

The Rat sits up straight.

Sam stands by the Rat's seat and puts his hand on the Rat's shoulder.

The Rat pulls away. "Don't touch me! What are you, gay or something?"

Sam slowly takes his hand off the Rat, sits down next to him, and looks at him seriously. "Would that matter to you?"

I know it is a genuine question. I see from the Rat's eyes and body language that it is a threat. It is as if he is a spider caught in a web. His skinny limbs are flailing, trying to get away, but he is stuck. The Incredible Hulk is blocking his way.

"Shit, just drive the damn bus, will ya?" The Rat is still squirming.

"Well, Richard—"

The Rat looks away when Sam says Richard.

"Richard, I'd appreciate it if you'd treat people with respect. This is our bus, and I'd like to keep it a safe and pleasant place."

Okay, Sam, you were doing well until now. That is weakling language you are using and the Rat can sniff a weakling.

Sure enough, the Rat's nose is twitching and his mouth is curling into a smile. He turns to Sam.

But Sam meets him halfway, leaning over so he is at the Rat's level, and puts his face right up to the Rat's.

The Rat jerks back. "Jeez, get your stinkin' breath away from me! You're a freak!"

Sam does not move. "That's not very respectful." His face is serious. "Do you know how to be respectful, Richard?"

Sam is still staring at him. The Rat keeps looking away. He cannot meet Sam's burning gaze.

Sam asks again, "Do you know how to be respectful?" Sam is about three times the size of the Rat. I realize how much I am enjoying noting this comparison.

The Rat squirms in his seat. He thinks Sam is threatening him with his Incredible Hulk size. I know that Sam is trying to perform another Quaker service, however misguided.

"Richard, do you need me to teach you about respect?"

The Rat squishes himself against the window. "I don't need you, man," he says, in a high squeaky voice.

"Are you sure? Because I'd like to help you."

"Just get away from me!"

Sam stays. His two hundred and fifty pounds stay. His piercing blue eyes stay. For a full minute. At least. While the Rat squirms.

Finally, Sam says, "Okay, then."

Sam gets up and the bus lurches again. He starts walking to the front of the bus.

"Freak," hisses the Rat.

Sam turns around and leans his hands on the seat backs on either side of him, bending forward. "Did you want to have that chat with me, Richard?"

The Rat does not answer.

"Or do I need to call your father and have all of us sit down together?"

I see the fleeting flicker of terror in the Rat's eyes. His

jaw goes slack and his face is even paler than usual. "No," the Rat squeaks.

I understand his fear. But not how he handles it. You will never control the violence with more violence. The Rat should have learned that by now.

"Okay, then." Sam heads to his seat.

The Rat mutters "asshole," but Sam does not hear. Perhaps the Rat believes he has won the battle since he got the last word in. But his slumped shoulders tell me that he knows he has lost this war. For the first time, I can look at him without fear. I breathe in deeply and exhale slowly. It is a pleasant change to be able to relax around the Rat.

The rest of the bus ride is silent. When we get to school my face is sore. It is twitching from tired muscles. I put my hand up to my face. And I realize what is happening. I am smiling.

CHAPTER TWENTY-SEVEN

The kid can now sit up by himself at the kitchen table. He can even crawl up onto a chair, a regular chair, not the high chair.

We sit down to dinner and he looks over at Sam's place, empty. "Saa–uh–Saa?"

"Sam is at a meeting, honey," Jessica tells him.

"Saaa." The kid sounds insistent.

Jessica pats his hand. "He'll be back soon."

"Saaa!"

"Sam is at a meeting." Jessica sounds like a broken record.

The kid pushes his plate and utensils over to Sam's spot and says, triumphantly, "Saaa!"

Jessica smiles. "Okay." She gets another place setting for the kid.

He is still not satisfied. He looks around and his eyes stop at the kitchen counter. "Saaa, Saaa, Saa–uh–Saa!" He shakes his hands excitedly and starts drooling.

"What do you want, Rory?" Jessica asks.

I get up and go to the counter. I see what he wants. *Green Eggs and Ham.* I hand him the book.

The kid shouts with glee and puts it at Sam's place. I know he is trying to stand it upright because he is moaning in frustration as it keeps falling flat.

I set it up for him, wedging it between the chair back and Sam's plate. The kid claps. "Tayyyy!"

Jessica smiles at me.

The kid keeps pointing to Sam's plate until Jessica puts food on it. Then he makes a sloppy of mess of feeding the book.

Jessica thinks it is adorable.

My throat gets tighter with every spoon of mashed potatoes that hits the orange cover. The sick tornado starts inside of me. Do you really not see the problem here, Jessica? The kid is too attached to Sam. That is a very bad thing. If he loses Sam, the kid could be completely destroyed.

And there has been another phone call to the Meeting House. About the peace vigils. And how they must stop.

The next night is Thursday. Sam puts on his baseball cap and grabs his puffy green vest.

I stare at him. "Must you go to the peace vigil every single time? You do realize your name is Sam Fox, not George Fox, right?"

"Saaa! Maaa!"

Jessica picks up the kid, who is reaching for Sam.

"See? Even the kid thinks you should stay home."

Sam has one arm in his vest and one arm out. "Uh . . . well, I'm kind of a regular, I guess." He grins and finishes plunging into his useless armor.

I fold my arms. "Are you really the only person who can lead the group? Surely someone else knows how to light a candle."

He stares at me for a moment, his forehead wrinkled, but then the wrinkles disappear and he winks. "But no one can sing like me!"

Jessica kisses Sam good-bye. I can see the worry in her eyes, too.

The man has too many meetings. Too many appearances. I cannot stand to think of the outcome, so I do not. I cannot bear the idea of watching the kid feed the Sam-book, either, but that I cannot ignore. So I ask Jessica if we can go out to dinner.

She looks at me questioningly.

"It can be somewhere cheap. I do not care. I will even eat a Happy Meal."

She furrows her brow for a moment but then nods her head. "Okay, let's go to Mel's, that little deli downtown."

I remember with a sinking feeling that Sam has the Subaru. Jessica has not realized this yet, apparently. There is no place to eat close by. We are stuck. I hold my breath.

"Bundle up!" she says. "It's a long walk, but the fresh air is good for us."

I breathe out and get my coat.

It is freezing. Jessica pushes the stroller over the ice-encrusted sidewalk and streets. I shiver, thinking how cold it must be to sit in a stroller.

When we finally get there, Jessica orders hot chocolate for all of us, even her. Probably they do not have raspberry tea at Mel's. I order a vegetable plate. Mashed potatoes and gravy, green beans, double order of applesauce.

"So," Jessica says, after working on feeding the kid his grilled cheese sandwich, "how's your dinner?"

"It is quite delicious. The chef is not as good as you, however."

Jessica is smiling at me. "Thanks."

I shrug. "I am just being Quakerly. Speaking the truth."

"Well, we try." She dabs her mouth with her napkin and smiles wryly. "It was quite a change for me, of course, being a lawyer."

"So you were a liar"—I do a fake cough—"oh, excuse me, I mean, a *lawyer* before becoming a Quaker?"

"Yes."

"Was it Sam who brought you over from the Dark Side to Quakerhood?"

She laughs. And her face turns pink. So the answer is obviously yes. "I suppose he helped. But I became a convinced Quaker—"

"A what? Is that like being converted?"

"No. Converted implies that someone else has persuaded you to adopt a certain viewpoint. Quakers don't do that. You explore and study the religion yourself. Then, if you're convinced it's right for you—"

"Then you are a convinced Quaker. But how did you become convinced?"

She smiles. "I guess I followed my Inner Light."

I am tempted to look around for some pretend spotlight.

"Jessica," I remind her, "when people are about to die, they see a light and follow it. If that is the light you are heading for, you might want to walk the other way."

She laughs but then her face turns serious. "You know, you have a very strong Inner Light yourself."

I roll my eyes. "Jessica, you have an oversensitive light detector."

"Me? Well, Sam says you have a blowtorch."

I roll my eyes. "Please! Do not try to make me into a Quaker."

"We're not trying to make you a Quaker, Matt. We're just trying to help you find a way to be happy."

For some reason, I cannot think of anything flippant to say, so I stare at the gravy on my plate for a while. Finally, I need to say something. "So, are we ordering dessert, or what?"

"Sure, what would you like?"

"Apple crisp."

Jessica laughs. "After a double order of applesauce?"

"Yes, it is apples in a completely different format."

"Well put." Then her face turns soft and serious and she stares at me for a moment. "You really like apple crisp, don't you?"

I think about it and finally decide that it is okay to tell Jessica the truth. "Yes."

"You know, I make a pretty good apple crisp myself. How about I make it on some First Day?"

I swallow. "That"—I try to speak in a monotone, not rude, but still not eager—"that would be nice."

Jessica smiles and looks at me like, well, like I believe a mother would. I am flustered and start shredding my napkin while I try to think of something to say to end the awkwardness. "I would still like it for dessert tonight, though."

"Apple crisp, it is! With ice cream?"

I shrug with relief. "All right."

Jessica orders the same thing for the kid. It is not a wise choice. His face is a sea of white foam with stubbly apple crumb rocks in it.

I look away.

Oh, my God.

It is him.

At a table. With the Wall.

The Rat.

I let out a scream. It is not a long scream. It is not a loud scream. And the diner is noisy. But it is still a scream and Jessica notices.

"What's wrong, Matt?" She turns around to look where I am staring.

"Turn around!" I whisper, crouching low over the table.

She does, and crouches, too. "What is it?" she whispers back.

"A . . . a . . . dork," I say.

Jessica and the kid both stare at me.

"From school. He's just a . . ." I do not understand why I am at such a loss for words. There is so much to say about him. Too much. "Dork," is all I can come up with. "Dork."

"I see." Jessica nods slowly, chewing her lip. "Well, we're finished, anyway. Shall I go take care of the bill?"

I nod.

As she slides out of the booth, the Rat looks over at us.

"Jessica!" I scream. I did not mean for it to come out like that.

She freezes.

"Um, perhaps you could get some LifeSavers. For Sam. Wintergreen. Please." In case he needs them.

Jessica straightens up and smiles. "Sure, Matt. Here, let me put Rory next to you while I go pay."

She places the kid on my bench. I am still staying low, out of the Rat's radar.

Jessica squeezes my shoulder. "I'll be right back, okay?"

I hear the Rat and the Wall, laughing. I wrap my arms around myself and mutter, "Shut up, dork."

The kid watches Jessica leave and looks at me. "Maa? Maa?"

I stare at him. I have no words to comfort him. I cannot even comfort myself.

He starts moaning, "Saaam, Saaa-uh-Saaam."

"Stop it!" I hiss. I do not want the kid using Sam's name. I do not want the Rat to make the connection.

The kid picks up a fork and starts banging the table. I try to get it away from him but he is too quick. He grabs some Domino sugar and Sweet'n Low packets and throws them in the air. I reach over him, trying to catch a pink packet, flailing at it, almost hitting the Rat.

Who is standing by our table.

Leering at me.

I gasp. And sink back against the wall. Then I stop breathing. I cannot even scream.

But I do something strange. I reach my arm around the kid. I actually touch him. Even with his sticky apple ice cream face. I pull him up against me and the gack touches my sweater. But that is better than letting the Rat touch him. I know it is. I will not let that happen.

"So, who's the retard?" He turns to the Wall, smirking.

I am staring at the Rat, clutching the kid, quaking.

The Rat turns back to us. "I mean, who's the *other* retard?"

I do not know what to do. I want to say, "Shut up, dork," to his face. But I do not want to die.

The Rat leans his greasy body over our table and sneers in my face. "Hey, moron," he hisses, "I'm getting suspended because you told Patterson about the booze. You're going to pay!"

I try to shake my head no because it was not me, but I cannot move. I cannot even raise my voice to summon Jessica.

I am stuck.

"Remember," the Rat sneers.

I am frozen.

"I'll get you."

I can smell his breath.

"When you least expect it." His spit hits my face.

"Shhh-uuup, dor!"

I jump.

The Rat flinches.

I turn to the kid with ice cream and apple crisp on his face. He is staring at the Rat. His face is red.

"Shhh-uuup, dor! Shhh-uuup, dor!" The kid is pounding the table with his little fist. And he is still staring straight at the Rat. Like he knows exactly what he is doing. I am staring at the kid in awe.

"What the hell is the little retard saying?"

I snap out of my awe and look at the Rat. He looks ready to pounce. I hold on to the kid even tighter.

But Jessica is here now, glaring at the Rat. "Please watch your language! And don't call my son by that name!" She takes a sharp breath and says, slowly, quivery, "His—name—is—Rory."

The Rat grunts, sneers at me with a Death Stare, and struts away. He goes back to the Wall, who are all laughing at him. He yells "shut up!" but they are still laughing.

Jessica's hands are shaking as she puts the kid in the stroller. The kid is still shouting, "Shhh-uuup, dor!"

"Shhh," says Jessica, through clenched teeth. She steps

hard on the stroller pedals several times before the brakes release, and she pushes off with a lurch. She looks at the Rat through narrowed eyes as she whisks the kid by his table. It is not a look of the Friendly persuasion.

The kid gets in one more, "Shhh-uuup, dor!" and the Wall laughs again.

Outside, Jessica walks very quickly down the sidewalk. I understand. Her adrenaline is still pumping. There is no place for it to go. I want to tell her that it is okay, that it will be better soon, but her face is too pinched to hear, I think.

I walk fast, trying to keep alongside her. Inside of me, a smile is growing. The Rat has just been dissed by the kid. The kid outsmarts the Rat. Maybe the kid is smarter than I thought.

While we are stopped at a street corner waiting for the stoplight to change, I look down at the kid. And I gently squeeze his arm through his parka. He looks up at me and grins. "Ayyy!" He claps his mittened hands.

It is hard not to smile back. At least a little.

By the time we stop at another intersection a few blocks later, the kid is yawning and his eyes are closed. Jessica taps her foot on the sidewalk, waiting for the light to change. When it does, though, she does not cross. Instead, she stares straight ahead. "Matt?"

She says it so softly I have to put my ear close to her to hear. "Yes?"

"Don't you think we should teach Rory some phrases other than 'shut up, dork'?"

I steal a look at her and see that her tight lips are spreading and the crinkly wrinkles around her eyes are growing.

Then she puts her arm around my shoulders, leans her head against mine, and bursts out laughing.

So do I. I do not remember the last time I laughed. It is a strange echo. It sounds like it is coming from far away, like someone else is laughing, not me. It is a nasal wheezing sound, like an asthmatic trying to catch enough breath but already too far behind. But it is not painful. At all. I think, perhaps, I could even get used to it.

CHAPTER TWENTY-EIGHT

I hear the phone ring downstairs and then Sam comes up to my room. His hands are in his pockets and his shoulders sag. "Matt, what's going on with you and Mr. Morehead?"

How did he find out? I sigh. "It was just one stupid detention."

Sam stands up straight. "Detention? For what?"

I stare at him. "I—I thought that was what you were talking about."

"No, I got a call from the office that you're failing the class. What's going on? And what's this detention about?"

I just shake my head. "He is an idiot."

"Did you . . . is that something you've told him to his face?"

"Oh, come on, Sam! I am not stupid! I do not actually say such things."

He is staring at me, biting his lip to hide a smirk.

"Okay, except to you. I would not say those things directly to a teacher."

"Then why—"

"It was Fatima."

"Who?"

"My term paper. I wrote it from the perspective of a Middle Eastern woman whose country was being invaded."

"And?"

"It was somewhat critical of the United States."

He takes his hands out of his pockets and pushes his hair back. "We're allowed to be critical. It's in the Constitution."

"Be careful, Sam, or Mr. Warhead will have you arrested for being a subversive."

"Mr. Warhead?"

"Actually, it is Mr. Morehead. I just call him that because it captures his personality."

Sam's lips twitch and he does a half smile. Then a whole one. "Okay, but let me understand this. He doesn't like the political views you expressed in your term paper, so he's failing you?"

I pick at my bedspread. "Well, it is not the only thing I have written that he does not like."

"What do you mean?"

"The man is a warmonger, Sam. He thinks I am not a patriot because I do not wish to invade other countries and create mayhem and murder. I tend to point out that perhaps we should leave other people alone. They might prefer peace." I shrug. "And somehow I drew a peace symbol on my desk."

"Beautiful." He says it quietly, but I hear him.

I look up.

His voice is still quiet. "I'm going to go see him."

"No! Sam, he is an idiot. He cannot be reasoned with."

He looks at me, his eyes piercing. "I will be fair. I will be reasonable. But I need to make my point."

"Are you insane? What makes you think he will even listen to you, much less change his mind? What do you think he is going to say?" I imitate Mr. Warhead's nasal voice. "Oh, you are right, Mr. Fox. I have been such an idiot. Thank you so much for showing me the Light." I give Sam my "you moron" look. "Do not even think of going to see him."

"Weren't you the one asking if I'd come to your school and talk about the peace testimony?"

"Excuse me?"

"When I was talking to that man in front of the Meeting House, you asked me why I couldn't—"

"Act like a normal person and go talk about peace at schools? Yes, but not my school, for God's sake."

"Why not?"

"Because someone other than you would be preferable."

"No, I would have to do it because—"

"You do not have to!"

"But this guy can't be allowed to persecute students for expressing their political beliefs. It's just wrong."

"So, it is wrong. Life is not fair, Sam. Get over it."

He is still shaking his head.

"Let it go, Sam."

He stares at me. "I can't let go. Not to things—and peo-ple—that matter this much to me."

I look away because his eyes are so piercing they hurt.

The next morning, Jessica is all teary. "I'm sorry about what you're going through with that . . . teacher." She is gritting her teeth, and I am sure she was thinking some un-Friendly curse word in between *that* and *teacher*.

"I wish Sam would just forget about it, for God's sake."

She nods. "I know. I'm afraid he can't." She is staring at

the table, her lips quivering, like she is going to start crying over the fact that the blue napkins do not match the mustard and mold kitchen.

"What?" I say.

She just shakes her head, blinks, and tries to make her quaking lips smile. "Toast?" she whispers, her eyes brimming. "Sorry, it's pretty burnt."

Why is she acting like this? She always burns the toast. It is not worth getting that upset about.

When I get on the bus, Sam says, all in one quiet breath, "Good morning, Matt. I'm seeing him after second period today."

I storm down the aisle and throw my backpack on a seat, then throw myself beside it. Great. Sam knows I cannot argue with him right here on the bus. I wish I had told him last night that, if he must see Mr. Warhead, to at least shut up about the Quaker connection. That will just put a big target on my head. I am not sure that detentions and extra-credit projects will be able to overcome the Quaker taint. Oh, Sam, why can't you just leave well enough alone?

I cannot help walking to Mr. Warhead's classroom after second period. Even though I have already had his class first period. The door is closed. I peek through the window.

I see Jessica, her face pinched, her eyes red. What is she doing here? Sam is leaning over with his elbows on his knees, but his head is held high and he is staring directly at Mr. Warhead, whose Hitler mustache is barely hiding his sneer. He looks like he can hardly wait to get rid of these Quaker pests. He gazes out the window, then to the whiteboard, then at the door. And he sees me. Why do I not run away? Oh, God, he is standing up and walking to the door. Sam and Jessica turn their heads to follow him and the door is open.

"You're part of this," Mr. Warhead says. "Have a seat!" He makes an exaggerated wave of his arm toward Sam and Jessica.

Sam gets up and lets me sit in his chair. He reaches for another one and his MIA bracelet jangles as he pulls the wobbly chair over.

"I have nothing against Quakers," Mr. Warhead says to Sam.

I glare at Sam. Why did he feel the need to share that with Mr. Warhead, for God's sake?

"But," Mr. Warhead continues, "I'm not sure it's appropriate for you to be proselytizing your religion to an impressionable young girl."

I switch my glare to Mr. Warhead. Who is he calling an impressionable young girl? The ass.

I see Sam clench his teeth but still smile. "We don't proselytize."

Mr. Warhead laughs his snorty nasal laugh. "Aren't you the ones who started the antiwar demonstrations? Not exactly supporting our troops, are you?"

"They're peace vigils," Jessica says.

Mr. Warhead's smile is so obviously fake. "Semantics."

"Semantics are everything," Jessica says, with no smile.

"Words can be very persuasive," Sam adds. "For example, 'You're either with us or with them' implies that you can't support peace and support our soldiers at the same time. But we do. We just want to stop the killing."

"Of our soldiers?"

"Of everyone."

Mr. Warhead leans forward in his chair. "So you want to save the enemy."

"I want to save human life. Why is that un-American?"

Mr. Warhead stares at Sam with his lips pressed together tightly. His eyes are burning into Sam.

Or, at least, they are trying to. Sam appears unaffected as he continues talking. "I'm very sorry about your son, Mr. Morehead. I—I can't even imagine what that must be like."

I steal a look at Mr. Warhead. He is blinking. His lips are smashed together. And his face is on its way to purple.

"I really admire and respect our troops," Sam says softly. "I just want them to come home."

"And I," Mr. Warhead replies through gritted teeth, "can't help but admire and respect the young people in my class who show concern for our troops and our country."

Oh, like the Rat? I want to say, "You are just being used! You are one of his victims!" but Mr. Warhead will refuse to see it, so why bother?

Sam is talking. Now Jessica. Defending me. And my views.

Jessica leans so far forward, she practically pounces on Mr. Warhead. "How dare you imply that she doesn't care? How dare you?" Sam reaches over and puts his hand on hers but she flashes him a glance almost as smoldering as the look she is giving Mr. Warhead. Sam slowly sinks back in his chair.

Jessica turns to Mr. Warhead again. "And even if she didn't—which I can tell you she most certainly does—how dare you let your emotions affect a child's grade? A child's future? That is an ugly abuse of power." She pauses. "Does your principal know about your biased attitude, I wonder?"

Mr. Warhead folds his arms and smiles a self-satisfied smile. "Jeff Patterson and I are old friends."

Jessica's eyes narrow. "Then perhaps we need to involve the school board." She is quite a force, this skinny little Quaker woman.

Mr. Warhead's smile turns into his usual tight-lipped grimace. He exhales loudly. "Well, thank you for your views. Now I understand why she's expressing them. Children often parrot what their parents say—or in this case, guardians."

"We're her parents," Jessica says, sitting forward in her chair again, at the same time Sam is saying "parents!" a little louder than is necessary. They both reach out for me and their warm hands are on mine.

Mr. Warhead gives them a condescending smile and looks at me. "I'm not going to hold your sarcastic remarks against you. I know you're only fourteen and haven't really developed a sense of who you are yet—"

"You don't know her very well, do you?" Sam breaks in.

Mr. Warhead shoots him a "shut up" look, as if Sam is one of his students.

"So I'll give you another chance, but you need to try to see both sides of the issue, not just keep parroting their views." He looks over at Sam and Jessica, wrinkling his nose like they are dog poop.

Me? Parroting their views? Ha! Where does he get off treating me like I am five? And have no brain? And what gives him the right to insult Sam and Jessica like they are ignorant five-year-olds, too? I feel my face turning toward him. I swallow. "Excuse me?" I say slowly.

"Well, I mean, you're not even a Quaker, right?"

I know the right answer. I know the answer that will let me pass this class. I know the answer that will let me graduate. And get to Canada. I hear myself saying, "A Quaker?" as if it is the oddest thing anyone has ever asked me.

Mr. Warhead smirks and nods, knowing that I am going to deny association with this cult.

But somewhere from deep within me, a rumbling comes to the surface and erupts out of my mouth with a "Hell, yes!"

Jessica closes her eyes. Her mouth is a straight, severe line.

Sam's is not. It is twitching. Back and forth. And up. Into a smile. Until he covers it with his hand.

Jessica stands up. "Well, we appreciate your doing the right thing, Mr. Morehead."

We walk out into the crowded hall. Jessica is tight-lipped and strained. Sam puts his hand out to shake Mr. Warhead's. Mr. Warhead is slow to respond and quick to stop shaking.

Several passing students call out, "Hi, Sam!"

Sam answers, calling each one of them by name. Mr. Warhead looks like he has eaten a lemon. No one says hi to Mr. Warhead.

"Hey! Sam!" a familiar voice calls.

"Rob, buddy! How are you?"

"Great!" Rob pushes through the crowd to shake Sam's hand.

"Rob, let me introduce you to my wife, Jessica."

Jessica smiles. "Hello, Rob. I've heard all kinds of nice things about you."

"Yeah?"

Mr. Warhead stares at all three of them. He looks like he has eaten three lemons.

I walk arm in arm with Sam and Jessica, one on either side of me. We form kind of a chain as we weave through the school connected like this. It is even stranger to walk through these halls without being frightened, without having to look for the Rat. In fact, I would almost enjoy meeting him right now.

At the front door, Sam and Jessica both give me a hug. I am not expecting that, so my attempts at return hugs are somewhat lame but they still smile at me. I stare after them as they walk down the front steps. I am not even embarrassed that they are holding hands.

Late that night, I hear Sam and Jessica talking quietly downstairs about the meeting with Mr. Warhead. I only catch a word or two here and there but when Sam says "that Matt!" I am desperate to hear more. I cannot resist putting my ear against the heat vent on my bedroom floor—the other side of which is conveniently located in the ceiling of their room. Why did I never think of this before?

Sam says I am "one smart, tough young lady." And he also says, "I love her spirit, don't you? She has such a strong spirit."

I sit up, lean against the bed, fold my arms, and smile. So. There you have it. Straight from the honest Alpha Quaker himself. I do not have a "smart mouth." Nor am I a "smart ass." Instead, I am simply "smart." And "tough." And I have a "strong spirit." A strong spirit. Who knew? It is a fresh persona for me. I am trying it on for size. I believe it fits. And I like it so much, I plan on keeping it.

CHAPTER TWENTY-NINE

The next morning, I get on the bus and say, "Good morning, Sam," before he can even say, "Good morning, Matt."

He grins big time.

I even shake his hand, feeling the jangle of the MIA bracelet that is a part of him.

I do not care if the Rat sees. He will not do anything to me on this bus. And this is the one day of the week I do not have World Civ. Today, right now, I feel safe.

In English, we get our papers back. Mrs. Jimenez has written all kinds of glowing things on my *Little House on the Prairie* paper. Her comments are about the feelings and the humor and the pain. They are real.

At the end of English, Mrs. Jimenez asks me to stay for a minute. I wonder if I am getting in trouble for my *Little House on the Prairie* paper, too, although I cannot imagine why.

"Matt, you're a wonderful writer. Very persuasive, too." She looks at me intently. I am waiting for the "but." "I've missed seeing you at the peace club meetings."

"Oh. That is because I am not actually a member. I just happened to be in the library that one day."

"Oh? Well, I was wondering if you'd be interested in working on our newsletter."

"Uh . . . why?"

She smiles. "We need to bring some different opinions into this school so we can have some debates, don't you think?"

I nod again. I am stunned that we think the same way.

"We're starting to distribute our newsletter around town—to the library, city hall, and various churches. You're a very persuasive writer and, I think, a very determined young woman. I'd love for you to be on our team."

Perhaps she is catching me in a rare upbeat moment, but I feel a thrill that I rarely remember feeling.

"Would you be interested?"

"I think so. Okay. Yes."

She is beaming so much I am almost blinded by her glow. I think she is about to hug me. "Could you stay after school next week? Monday? We're having a special meeting just of the web designers and newsletter editors."

Her happiness is so contagious, I cannot help but smile. And nod.

I am floating through the day on a cloud, as if Maggie Mahone's shawl is the Quaker Cloak and nothing can go wrong.

Until I get on the bus in the afternoon and there is no Sam.

Where is Sam? I am not feeling invincible anymore.

Other people are asking the bus driver where Sam is. The man does not know. Or is not telling. By the time Rob gets on the bus and asks the driver, for maybe the tenth time, the guy yells, "I'm just a sub, all right? What do I know?"

I cannot wait until I get to my stop. The Rat is way too

happy. He is tripping and punching people. The bus driver does nothing.

Finally, I get off. And run all the way to the house, bursting in, out of breath. "What happened to—"

Sam is standing there. Leaning against the kitchen counter. Holding Jessica. Who is crying.

"Hi, Matt," Sam says with a soft smile.

Jessica straightens up and wipes her eyes, giving me a wobbly smile. "Hi, honey."

The kid is hugging both of them around the ankles. "Maaa."

"I lost my job," Sam tells me.

"What! Why?"

Sam takes a deep breath. "I never registered for the Selective Service."

I am about to demand more of an answer when I start to figure it out for myself. I remember reading about this on Sam's blog.

I look at Jessica. She knew he would lose his job. That is why she was so upset yesterday morning. It was not the burnt toast.

She smiles weakly and bends down to pick up the kid.

I drop my backpack. "I told you not to go see Mr. Warhead! He snitched, right? He figured it out because you are a Quaker or because of everything you said to him about peace. And afterward, in the hall, he found out that you were a bus driver. Bingo. A government job. Which you lose— even now—if you do not register with the Selective Service, right?" I shake my head. Sam. Sam.

Sam shrugs. "It may not have been him. It may have been a routine check."

"A routine check? Oh, come on, Sam!"

"Well, I didn't mark the box on the employment application about Selective Service. I just left it blank. Maybe somebody noticed."

I roll my eyes.

Sam hangs his head. "I know. I—I didn't feel good about submitting an application that was incomplete. It was deceptive. That's the same as a lie. I should never have applied. I just . . . well . . . really wanted the job." He sighs. "I'm not proud of myself."

I stare at him. "I am not disgusted with you, for God's sake. I am mad at Mr. Warhead! You did not do anything wrong, Sam!"

"Well, it was deceptive not to mark the box."

"It was their fault for not reading the stupid form, then!"

He shakes his head.

"Sam, you were the best bus driver! You were a—a role model! Everyone missed you today! Everyone asked about you!"

"And now they'll know what I did was wrong. What kind of a role model is that?" His shoulders droop.

"Oh, for God's sake, get over it, Sam! Do you not feel the least bit upset that something was taken away from you that should not have been?"

Sam starts to answer, but Jessica interrupts. "I agree with Matt."

Sam jerks and stares at her.

She pushes the kid's hair out of his eyes. "You took a stand, Sam. You don't need to feel sorry about that."

"This totally sucks," I say.

Jessica nods. She does not even tell me to watch my language. "I'm going to take Rory up for a bath."

Sam gives them a hug before they leave. Then he sighs and sits down at the kitchen table. He fingers a blue napkin and for a moment I think he is going to shred it like I do.

I sit down next to him and stare at him. "Okay, this is what I do not understand. Why does God, in his infinite wisdom, let stuff like this happen?"

He exhales slowly. "I don't know. But I believe a way will open."

"What? Is that another Quaker thing?"

He nods. "You'll get an idea and you'll know immediately, at a gut level, that it's the right thing. Sort of like a door opening and you realize, that's it."

"As in, I have seen the Light!"

"Something like that."

"Well, that must be very nice and comforting for those of you who see some Light, but it makes no sense to the rest of us." Just because I told Mr. Warhead I was a Quaker does not mean I am for real. God!

Sam smirks, flicks his thumb against his clenched fingers, and holds them up to his other fist, then makes a *whoosh* sound.

"What is that supposed to mean?"

"Don't you know a blowtorch when you see one?"

I roll my eyes but I wonder if a way will open if you are not Quaker. Or if I would even recognize a way if one opened in front of me.

I decide to share my plan with Sam. "How about moving to Canada?"

He gives me a quizzical look, like perhaps I am being sarcastic.

"I am serious."

"But . . . this is my home, Matt. And I can't run away."

"Why not?" It is not a flippant remark. It is a genuine question. I want to know.

"Because everyone I know and love is right here. I'm privileged to be an American. I'm privileged to live right here."

"You are not looking so privileged at the moment, Sam."

"But I have the right and the power to make a difference."

"I believe that exists in Canada, also. And it may be an easier battle."

He takes a deep breath, looks at the floor, then looks at me. "I ran away to Canada before. I'm not doing it again."

"Excuse me?"

"When I didn't want to sign up for Selective Service. I ran away. I hid."

Sam? Sam ran away? The websites—all those bookmarked sites—flash through my head. His blog. For kids who did not sign up for Selective Service. Of course he could help them. He was an expert.

I look at him and he wipes his hand over his mouth. "It just didn't make any sense to me. Went against everything I believed. Our whole reason for being there was wrong. Peacekeeping is one thing, but . . . So, one morning I decided to hitchhike as far away as I could get." He stares off into the distance. "Up through New York, into Ontario and along the TCH—the Trans-Canada Highway—into Quebec, through New Brunswick, and all the way into

Nova Scotia. I worked at a sawmill and on a commercial fishing boat. It's beautiful up there. Beautiful people, too. But I learned something." He looks down at his hands and rubs his MIA bracelet. "About myself. About who I am and where I belong. Canada's great. But I'm not Canadian. I'm American, and this is where I belong. I decided to never run away again." He looks up at me. "I'm going to stay right here. And work on making things better."

As the shock of this news wears off, I feel a tingling, like after my fingers are numb from being out in the cold for a long, long time, and they start to burn when they finally thaw. My head feels prickly, almost painful, as if it, too, is thawing. And I wonder, is it possible to run away from things but then turn around and face them again? Sam ran away. But then he came back. And he has been back ever since. Could it work for me? To not run? Not hide? Face everything?

Sam grabs my hand and squeezes it. For some reason, I do not throw him off. "I think that's what we should do," he says softly, staring into space. "Work on making things better."

I let him sit there, holding my hand. For a long time. In silence. Just being.

When he finally lets go, my hand is cold and exposed, and its bareness makes my whole body shudder.

CHAPTER THIRTY

From my bed, I hear the muffled voices of Sam and Jessica downstairs. I can hear Jessica crying. I wonder what they are saying. I am hoping they are coming up with a plan to reinstate Sam as bus driver. But it is unlikely.

The kid hears them, too. He keeps calling, "Maaa!"

Finally, I get up and go to his doorway. Jessica has enough to worry about right now.

He is standing in his crib and holding on to the bars. He can barely see over the top. "Maaa!" He sounds even louder now.

I remember not to say, "Shut up, dork," because it is not good training for him. Except when speaking to the Rat. So I say, "Shhh." It sounds stupid and noisy. I do not know why this is used as a sound to quiet people down. It is irritating and grating. And loud.

"Maaa!"

And it does not work.

I whisper, "Quiet, okay?"

He seems to understand. "Maaa," he whispers back.

Now what? "Uh . . . you really should go to sleep."

He starts saying, "Maa, maa, maa," rapidly now, though

still quietly. There is another sound in his mantra that I cannot quite make out, at the end of one "maaa" before he goes on to the next, as if he is marking the ending.

I walk into his room, lit by the blue glow from his star lamp. I look around, realizing that I have never actually stepped inside his room before. There is a white chest of drawers with a blue towel on top where they change his Pull-Ups, a rocking chair, a huge stuffed bear in the corner, and the crib. That is all because there is no room for anything else.

The kid is still saying his "maa, maa, maa" mantra and I remember that I have walked inside to figure out his new sound. It is something that would make Sam and Jessica happy. Maybe he is trying to say "Maam." Maybe it will eventually turn into "Mom."

It does not sound like "Mom" yet. He is not making an *M* sound at the end. It is a sound from inside his mouth, more like a *D*. Mad? He would not say "mad." No, it is almost as if the sound is catching in his throat, cutting the "Maa" short.

"Ma—Ma—"

But he is clearly doing it on purpose. In fact, he is staring at me, his big eyes earnest and his little forehead all wrinkled. "Ma—" He puts one arm over the bars of the crib, pushing his hand toward my chest.

I am not sure what he wants.

He takes a deep breath, stares into my eyes, and points his finger straight at me. "Ma—!" he shouts, and points at me again. "Ma—!"

Oh, my God.

It is me.

He is saying *Matt*.

My mouth is hanging open and I am staring at him now, into his eyes. But I cannot move.

He blinks his eyes and lifts up his arms toward me. "Maa—, Maa—, Maa—"

My eyes are stinging and my throat is burning. Still, I cannot move.

"Maa—, Maa—" His little hands are opening and closing as if trying to grab on to something. They are almost touching me.

I snap out of my frozen state, lurch forward, and shake the crib side. I push on levers and shake and yank. Nothing moves. "I do not know how this stupid thing works!"

"Maaa—" His arms are reaching up and his hands are touching my shoulders.

I reach into the crib, put a hand under each of his arms, and lift him out.

He is heavier than my backpack. And softer. And I do not know how to make him stick to me the way he sticks to Jessica and Sam.

But he knows because he immediately wraps his short arms and legs around me and I am sure he would not fall off even if I let go. Which I will not.

I am feeling suddenly tired, so I sit down in the rocking chair. It starts moving front and back, like we do.

His little body is warm and heavy and soft, all at the same time. He is even better than Maggie Mahone's shawl. He is comfort.

He smells like raspberries. Jessica's hand lotion. Jessica's tea. And he has his own smell, too, a good smell, of clean pj's and orange books and blue pots and I breathe it in deeply.

He touches my hand, stroking it and making gurgling sounds that turn into a gentle "Maa—" He looks up at me and smiles and I feel trust. He wraps his hand around my forefinger and squeezes it and bends his head down and I hear his kiss.

We rock back and forth, his head resting on my heaving chest and my head resting on his and we make gurgling and heavy breathing noises together.

"Maa—tayyy?"

I lift my head from his and stroke his warm soft hair. I sigh. It is not okay. Not at all. But I decide not to say that. "Yes, it is okay. Rory."

He lifts his head up from my chest and stares at me. I stare back. It is the first time I have said his name. His smile is so big he looks like Sam.

My eyes are burning. My face is wet. It makes my skin prickly and itchy. I do not know why I am acting this way.

Except that Sam has lost his job. And Jessica is still crying. And I think it is all my fault. And I am failing Mr. Warhead's class. And the Rat is making my life miserable. And life is so unfair. And I cannot see the way.

And Rory said my name.

CHAPTER THIRTY-ONE

There is a different sub driving the bus the next morning. I sit right behind the driver because the Rat is only a few seats back and his feet are blocking the way across the aisle. I shake the rain off of me but I keep my shawl over my head to block out the Rat.

When Susan gets on the bus, she stops after a few steps.

I pick up my backpack, put it on my lap, and slide over to the window.

She rushes to my seat. "Thanks, Matt," she whispers.

I am so shocked at the sound of my name that I turn to look at her. She has a tiny face with hair that hides most of it. And a small nose with freckles. And a sweet smile.

"I didn't want to have to walk past . . . ," she mumbles, jerking her head toward the Rat.

"I understand. Susan." I make myself say her name since she said mine.

Her smile grows. "Thanks."

Later, Rob stops me in the hall. "Hey, Matt. Did you hear about Sam? The bus driver?"

"Um . . . why . . . what did you hear?"

"My uncle's a bus driver. He said Sam broke some law or something, but I can't believe it. He was a good guy—"

"He is a conscientious objector, for God's sake! He did not register for the Selective Service. That is all!"

Rob steps back and puts his arms up. "Whoa! I'm on his side, okay? I didn't know that was it. That's so bogus. How—how do you know about this?"

"He is a . . ." I do not know what to call Sam. "A friend." I say it with a lowercase *f* because that is what I mean.

"Friend?"

"And sort of like a . . . parent, I guess."

His eyes get big. "Whoa. That explains it."

Excuse me? "Explains what?"

"That's how he knows so much about you."

"What do you mean?"

He shrugs. "Just stuff."

Stuff? Like what stuff? And why is Rob looking at me like that? Disapprovingly.

"You never even talk to him on the bus."

I think about how much Rob talks to Sam, and I look at the floor.

"He's a good dude. You know, some bus drivers—some adults—don't want to deal with you at all if you're in high school. Sam actually talks and listens and treats us like we're equals."

He is right. I know. I am still staring at the floor.

"But I guess it's hard having your dad be the bus driver, huh?"

"No," I say quickly. "Actually, it is not hard at all." And I think how easy it really is, compared to what your dad could be.

"Wait a minute. Is he a Quaker? Because that would make sense. Their religion won't let them fight."

I squirm. "That is not exactly true. Their religion does not dictate anything. It is their choice what they do. But they believe in peace, which tends to make it difficult to go to war."

He turns his head slightly as his brown eyes look at me, as if he does not know what to expect next. "Okay," he says, unzipping his backpack and pulling out a notebook, "I'm starting a petition to reinstate him as our bus driver."

"It will not work."

Rob stops, glaring at me. "What, don't you think he has a right to be a conscientious objector?"

"It does not matter what I think. It is simply the law."

"Well"—he exhales, looking at me like I am a moron—"then you change it."

"It is not that easy."

"Yeah? Well, nobody said life is easy. Are you just going to lie down and let people walk over you?"

I watch him as he gets out a pen and writes across the top of a page in his notebook. He draws determined lines down the page, dividing it into columns. He looks up at me as I watch him. His jaw is set. His mouth is resolute. And his eyes are staring at me. "What?" There is an edge to his voice.

"I am waiting . . . to sign the petition."

"Oh. Okay." The hard edge is gone. He hands me the notebook and pen. "Do you want to be first?"

Number one? At the top of the list? Where there is no hiding? From the Rat? Or Mr. Warhead? Or anyone else? Is he crazy?

"Yes," I hear myself say. And I print my name large. And my address. Which happens to be the same as Sam's.

As I head up the stairs to English, I see the Rat and the

Wall. They are talking with Mr. Warhead, who is red-faced. The Rat is obviously arguing with him, like he really cares about something or really cares about what Mr. Warhead thinks or both. The Wall looks bored or disgusted, depending upon where you look. Mr. Warhead shakes his head no and folds his arms. He stares at the Rat for a moment before walking into his classroom.

The Rat's shoulders fall. He shakes his head, too, but it is the fed-up kind of head shaking, and he hits the door frame with his fist. Then he turns away.

I do not take evasive action in time and the Rat's eyes trap mine. I am only a few steps away from him now and I try to turn around, but I am on the wrong side of the hallway for that. So many people are pushing me forward that I cannot even slow down.

In seconds his camouflage jacket blocks my way and the Wall surrounds me. I smell his smoke. His sneer and hiss are quiet but still forceful. "You're dead . . . Quaker!"

I am cold all over. He knows. I am dead. It really is over.

The tornado rises inside me and my entire body is a quivering mass. I almost choke from cigarette smell and his camouflage jacket fills my view. Daggerlike strands of greasy hair slice the air in front of my face. His crooked nose twitches. His black eyes skewer me as I stand there, fresh, raw meat, and I want to look away but I am hopelessly impaled. His huge face is in front of me and I try to breathe but he has all the air and there is none left for me and I am dizzy.

"Chicken-shit!" the Rat yells in my face, and I clutch my chest but I leave a chink exposed and his elbow catches my rib. He shoves me and I fall to the floor.

I huddle on the floor with my backpack. His boot steps

on my skirt, squashing it slowly like he is wiping his foot on a mat. And then the smoke smell dissipates and a trail of boots and laughter follow and when I am sure they are gone, I get up slowly, stiffly, and stagger in the other direction.

I sit numbly through Biology. As sixth period draws near, I feel sick all over. I know why. It is time for World Civ. I cannot stand the idea of facing Mr. Warhead. Or the Rat.

So I go to the nurse's office. "I cannot handle this awful period," I tell her, doubled over. I mean sixth period, but she assumes it is the other kind and lets me lie down.

A few minutes before the final bell is due to ring, the nurse tells me to go to my locker so I will not have to push through the crowds. She is very considerate, this nurse. She reminds me of Jessica.

At my locker, I am shaking. I am thinking I have made myself sick by feigning illness. Perhaps it serves me right. Or perhaps I have picked up some fast-acting germs from the nurse's office. Perhaps, I shudder, feeling a darkness moving toward me, it is the Rat.

As soon as I see him at his locker, I know he is not getting on the bus. I am sure of it. But how? An Immaculate Perception?

I am shaking. If he is not getting on the bus, I should be happy. I am safe. Everything is good.

But it is not, and I know it.

I walk slowly out to the bus, looking back constantly to see the Rat, as if I cannot quite leave him behind.

Something is wrong. He is outside in the parking lot now, standing with the Wall, the older guys who have the beat-up car. They are whispering and guffawing and punching each other's arms.

The Rat is smoking a cigarette and the quaking begins. I shake my head to try to drive out the growing fear. It does not work. Why do I think something is wrong, anyway? They are only exhibiting their usual moronic behavior.

All I want to do is get on the bus and hide. Shut my eyes. Shut myself off.

So I do.

"Hi, Matt."

I jump. It is Susan, smiling, sitting down next to me.

"Oh." I swallow. "Hi."

She starts to say something, but Rob plunks himself down on the seat in front of us, sideways, so he is looking over the seat back. He hands Susan the petition.

As the bus drives off, I see the Rat get into the car. I hold my breath.

"Wow, you were the first to sign it." It is Susan again, holding the petition.

"Yes." My eyes are following the car. It starts. I turn around in my seat to see where it goes.

"What is it?" Rob asks.

I try to look at him, instead of the car, which is turning the opposite way out of the parking lot. "Nothing. I am sure it is nothing."

His intense eyes are looking at me. They are the kind of eyes that can see into you if you give them a chance. I look away.

Someone calls to him and he goes into his petition speech, dragging Susan into the conversation, too. I crane my neck behind me to see if I can find the Rat's car. Nothing.

I try to focus on what is going on in the bus. It is the first time Susan speaks at great length. With Rob. With anyone.

For a fleeting moment I wonder if all the Robs and all the Susans and all the Matts could band together and defeat the Rat and his Vermin.

But it is my stop and I jump up.

"Bye, Matt," says Susan.

Rob pats my backpack as I walk past his seat. "See you tomorrow."

Tomorrow? I look at him. And say nothing. God knows what will happen by tomorrow.

CHAPTER THIRTY-TWO

I run to the house. Fast. Maybe the something wrong is happening there. Right now. Maybe it is Rory. Or Jessica. Or Sam.

There is no Subaru out front. I can see no lights on in the house. I run up to the door and turn the handle. It is unlocked. I throw it open. "Sam? Sam!"

Why am I calling his name?

The house is empty. I flick on the lights in the hall and kitchen, and drop my backpack on the floor.

I see a note on the kitchen table. It is Jessica's handwriting on a scrap of paper.

> *Dear Matt,*
> *I have to take Rory to the doctor for a physical. We'll pick Sam up at his meeting on the way home. Back around 6 pm.*
> *Love you,*
> *Jessica*
>
> *P.S. Can you guess what we're having for dessert? I couldn't wait for a First Day.*

There are six apples on the counter. And a stick of butter. And a glass pan. And an index card, yellowed and worn on the edges. In old lady cursive it says "Apple Crisp."

She is making apple crisp. To me. For me. Because of me.

I should be happy. But somehow I am in more pain than ever. Why does caring have to hurt? I never meant to get involved.

I look at the clock on the stove. It is 4:02. The second hand is creeping around so slowly I know it will never get to 6:00. And I realize now why I hate this clock. It is just like the clock on the stove when I was little. I remember watching it. Waiting for my father to get home. It is how I learned to tell time. I was an expert at knowing how many minutes of peace were left in the day. I have the same bubbly feeling inside of me. It is not excitement. It is not happiness. It is the dread of certain horror. Because I know something bad is going to happen.

I take a deep breath, try to calm down. I look up and notice, for the first time, that the rainbow peace flag is folded up on top of one of the kitchen cabinets. No one will attack this house, then. No one will know there are peace lovers inside. So why am I still quaking?

I look outside. It is already gray on its way to dark. I pick up a napkin and start shredding. What is happening out there? What are the Rat and his gang doing? I do not want to think about it. I just want to go upstairs to bed.

But my whole body is prickly, quaking, and I know I could not sleep even if I hid under a hundred blankets. Or under the bed. I have shredded my napkin completely. I pull a paper towel off of the roll and rip it into tiny bits until there is a pile of white flakes in front of me. Like snow.

The tornado inside me is twisting. I look at the clock. It is 4:06. The phone rings and I scream. Then I grab it. And the person hangs up before I even say anything. Is it a sign? I want to jump out of my skin.

I pace jerkily around the kitchen, knocking over a chair. Where is the Rat now? What are they doing? It is something. It is something bad. I know it. But I am the only person in the world who knows. Why did you have to get fired, Sam? You would have known something was wrong. You could have stopped him.

Why are you guys leaving me alone with this? It is not fair. Not right. If you "love" me, Jessica, why are you out with Rory instead of being here for me? See, it is all too confusing. I should never have gotten involved.

I am angry. I cannot stay in this darkening house by myself any longer. I have to see what the Rat is up to.

It is an insane idea. What can I do? I do not even know where he is.

Except I can guess. By the way the car turned out of the parking lot. Toward the only place I have seen them outside of school. Mel's. They are at Mel's. Scheming. Scheming to hurt someone.

I start to sit down at the computer and I see half a roll of wintergreen LifeSavers next to the keyboard. I jump up again. Sam should have his LifeSavers with him. He is at the Meeting House, for God's sake! What is he thinking?

I am tripping over the furniture and walking into counters because I am pacing so hard.

I need to pace outside.
I slam the door behind me.
And I walk.
Quaking.
To Mel's.

CHAPTER THIRTY-THREE

My boots are heavy. My legs are rubber. It is not a good combination.

The sidewalk feels hard and jarring, like it is sending pain on purpose ringing through my calves, jolting my knees, and punching my back.

I shiver convulsively and realize that I am not wearing my jacket. I do not even have Maggie Mahone's shawl. It is only March. Why did I come out with just a shirt? I feel a biting cold, pain, and stinging that I do not remember feeling for a long time. But it is too late to turn back. It is almost dark.

I turn onto the main road, the cars and trucks speeding past me. Their headlights shine in my face, hard and cold. Boring inside my brain to examine me, see if I am crazy, see if I am permanently damaged. Like the doctor's intense beam straight into my eyeballs on my fifth birthday. After my happy birthday concussion. From my father.

I choke on the diesel fumes from the trucks. And all the exhaust fumes. I smell the wood smoke from someone's fireplace. Someone who is inside, safe and warm. And I wonder, Why am I out here?

The traffic sprays me with icy water. The air from the

speeding cars is like a fan on high, producing painful wind-chill. I shudder and keep walking my jerky, spastic, quaking walk.

A truck horn blasts and I see the deer, frozen in the road for a split second before I look away. I do not want to see it run over. I hear the air brakes but no thud. I look back to see the deer running past the trees on the other side of the road.

Then a horn honks at me. Loudly. I jump to the side. I was not even on the road, for God's sake. The driver of a pickup shouts out his window, "Careful, sweetheart!" I shudder and move on.

I finally approach an intersection where cars are stopped and I am passing them for a change. I hear the bass from a car stereo, even with the windows up. The noise gets under my skin, in my blood, through my bones. It makes me quake more.

The traffic starts up and a minivan passes. The kid inside has the light on and is reading a book. The interior of another minivan is lit up by headlights. I see two kids laughing and throwing things at each other. In an old car, a mother is obviously lecturing her daughter. Who is lecturing back.

Signs of life. But none of them has any idea what is about to happen.

Neither do I.

Maybe I am just going to Mel's for a cup of hot chocolate. To warm me up. I am just going there because there is no one at home and I need a place to go for a little while. That is all.

No, I know it is more than that. I know this feeling. It comes straight from my gut, bypassing my brain. It is my Early Warning System.

And it is never wrong.

I round the corner. I can see Mel's down the street. I stop. And wait. Frozen. I do not want to see what is going on inside. This is stupid. Senseless. I turn to go back but my feet will not move. They are one with the sidewalk, riveted to the feeling of a hundred million footsteps that came before them. I look back at Mel's and stare for a minute. Two minutes. Too many minutes.

The Rat and the Wall flow out of Mel's like blood oozing from a gaping wound.

I shrink against the corner building and try to blend in. They are standing there doing their stupid rituals. Slapping each other on the back. Lighting a cigarette. Throwing the match on the sidewalk. Someone mutters something and they laugh. The biggest guy pulls a beer bottle out of his jacket, and the group goes into a huddle like they are playing football. I cannot hear anything they are saying, but I watch. And wait.

Finally, the Rat punches his fist in the air. They laugh and trail down the street away from me.

I watch them. Walking off. My feet turn. And start to follow. I do not want this. I do not need this. But I cannot stop.

I follow at a distance the ugly scourge that is the Rat and his gang. They reach their car and get in, two in the front, three in the back, and drive to the next street, and make a right. Out of sight.

I run, trying to catch them, and realize that it is insane for me to run after them when they are in a car. How will I ever keep up?

I am gasping for air when I reach the corner and turn right and cannot see the car.

And then I do. It is several blocks down, on the left, at a gas station. I walk to catch up, but not get too close, still watching. The lights above the pumps are harsh but they do not make things look bright. The Wall is not filling up the tank. They are pumping gas into a small gas can. Now one of them has gone inside the building. The others gather around the trunk, put the gas can inside, but look around them, as if hiding something else inside the trunk.

They are still a block ahead of me when they leave the station. Slowly. Now two blocks. I start to run again. Block after block. The traffic lights slow them down so I can still see them. Sometimes I get too close and stop and look away. Scared that they will turn around and see me. Scared that I will turn around and lose them. Scared of what they are about to do.

And it is when we get to the next street and they turn left and I pick up my pace so as not to lose them that I finally figure out where we are. And what they are going to do. And who they are going to hurt.

I can see the lights inside the Meeting House from here.

My legs stop. My breath is rasping, grasping for air. The scream dies in my throat. My tears are the only things moving and they burn my cheeks.

Surely the Rat and the Wall will drive on. Surely they are not going to do the unthinkable. Surely, no.

But they do not move on. They park the car on the same side of the road as the Meeting House. The driver stays in the car, keeps the engine running. The others get out and go to the trunk. I hear the clank of bottles, probably beer, and a "shhh!"

And then I see what they are doing. They are filling the bottles with gas from the can.

My throat is so blocked now I cannot scream. I cannot even whisper. No sound will come out. My whole body is shaking, quaking.

They are putting rags in the bottles.

Finally, I move my head. Forward. Trying to break through the invisible barrier. My feet follow. Slowly. I am trying to run, but it is like I am in a nightmare. I am barely shuffling, disabled by what, I do not know, but I can hardly stay upright and it is a struggle to move forward.

Scream! I have to warn Sam. In case I cannot get there in time.

"Sa—!" It comes out as a squeak. It does not even sound like "Sam."

I swallow, breathe in a raspy breath, "Saaa," and cannot finish. But I make myself keep saying it. Like Rory. Over and over. Louder and louder. "Saaa, Saaa, Saa-uh-Saa, Saaam!"

And I am moving faster now. I am getting closer to the Meeting House. "Sam! Sam! Get out!" I have to run right past them but I do not care.

I hear a shout. I see some of them move. Toward me. Fast.

But I do not stop.

I keep going, running, forcing myself to look only at the Meeting House windows, only at the light—

I feel a shove from behind, flinging me forward, landing me on the sidewalk so hard that I hear a loud crack from the side of my face. Afterward, it is silent.

Until I hear singing coming from the Meeting House. I recognize it. The George Fox song.

Angry and scared voices hiss behind my head, above me.

"What do we do?"

"Put her in the bushes!"

"Just get her out of here."

"Do you think anyone heard?"

"Shut up!"

"Is she dead?"

"I said shut up!"

I feel the wetness from the sidewalk creeping through my shirt, icing my stomach, chest, and arms.

Someone shoves me and rolls me over like I am a sack of potatoes. He can kick as hard as he wants but he cannot destroy what is inside. I have a strong spirit and the Rat will never take that away from me, no matter what he does.

And I realize why they might think I am dead. I am still not breathing. My eyes are closed. And I am not struggling. Good. Let them think I am dead.

It is hard not to gasp for air. But I have done harder things. I think of George Fox and I know, like him, I can do this. They push me under some bushes. The twigs of the bushes stab my chest and scratch my face. It hurts. Still I do not open my eyes. I am about to pass out from not breathing. I want so badly to gasp a breath of air.

And they are gone and I gulp and wheeze, trying to get air into my lungs, past the pain of my winded chest, when I hear the muffled voices of the Wall and I know I have to move. Now.

I am crawling, freeing myself from the bushes. I struggle to my knees, pushing myself forward. It is excruciatingly slow. But I am moving. I am getting closer.

The singing ends.

Out of the blackness I see the flicker from a lighter.

And suddenly everything is clear and I see how close I am and I scream. "Sam! Sam! For God's sake, get out, Sam!"

A light turns on outside the Meeting House, shining on the steps and the path up to it. It also lights up the faces of the Rat and the Wall, holding their flaming gas-filled bottles. They are all frozen for a minute like people dancing in one flash of a strobe.

"Sam! Bombs! Get out!" I scream loudly.

The door opens. And it is Sam.

Someone shouts, "Now!" and there is a spark, a flying flame, a crash of glass, a flash of light, the smell of gas, and fire.

Where Sam used to be.

He is gone.

CHAPTER THIRTY-FOUR

I am screaming.

I get up and try to run but my feet are frozen stumps and I stumble to the ground. My numb hands will not push me upright so I shove forward with my knees and try to pull with my elbows. My knees and elbows scrape the path, shredding, but I do not care. I need to get to Sam. Please let me get to Sam.

People run down the steps. I can see the Quaker feet. I am lifted up.

"Matt! It's Matt! Are you okay?"

I squirm and scream, guttural noises that do not sound anything like "Sam," but they know what I mean.

"We've got him," a man's voice says.

"It's all right," a woman's voice tries to tell me.

And then more voices behind me. "There they go!" I hear a car engine revving and tires squealing.

"I can't read the license plate!"

"It's an old Chevy! I can tell by the taillights!"

"I'm going after them!"

The voices get fainter as I am carried up the steps of the Meeting House. People are stamping out glowing embers on the concrete porch. A woman clutches a fire extinguisher, spraying dust around the front door. I smell burned wood.

I look around wildly for Sam but I cannot see him.

A man holds a cell phone to his ear and tugs on his hair with his other hand. "One casualty. We need an ambulance fast."

Casualty? *Casualty?* What does he mean?

"Sam!" I scream.

I am standing in the hallway now. I turn toward the Meeting room, take a step, and fall flat. They are there, holding my arms, picking me up again. Someone puts a large jacket around my shoulders. I hear people saying, "Matt!" I see Laurie's face in front of me and she pushes the hair out of my eyes. But I want Sam.

I press forward into the Meeting room and there is a crowd of people in the center of the circle of metal chairs and I know Sam is in the middle of them but I cannot seem to get there.

I hear his name being screamed but this time it is not me. It is Jessica.

I turn and see her running through the doorway with Rory in her arms. Her face is wild and her hair looks gray as death. Rory is screaming, "Sam-I-Saaaaam!"

Jessica dashes into the circle and drops to the floor and I know she has found Sam. I stumble and try to get there, too. It takes forever. Why does it take so long? I push through the crowd of people.

I hear Rory again. "Sam-I-Saaaam!" Then, "Maa—!" He sees me, and reaches his arms up to me.

I try to answer but I can only squeak. I reach my arm out

to him but there are a million people in between us. Jessica looks up. She is crying. She reaches one hand out to me, above the crowd. Finally. I have a target and can move straight, fast, toward her.

I drop down by her side. I feel her hand on my face. But I see her other hand on Sam's chest. I see his sweatshirt. It is intact. Then I smell the acrid, singed, burning smell, and I am scared to look at his face. If it is there.

My eyes are cloudy. Is his face a murky mess, or is it my eyes?

I hear sirens. I do not want them to come. Please, God, do not let them take him away! Please, God, let him live.

"Saam-I-Saam!"

For Rory's sake, let him live.

Jessica sobs.

For Jessica's sake.

The sirens are louder.

For my sake.

I hear the paramedics' radios crackling.

Please make them go away!

"Over here!" someone calls. The radios get louder. And I can hear the stretcher coming.

No! Please go away!

"It's all right, Matt," I hear a man's voice saying, softly, quietly, shaky, quaking.

"No." I shake my head through my tears. "No, nothing is all right."

"But I'm okay," he says, and he pushes himself up on one elbow with a groan. His other Michelin Man arm comes around me. "I'll be fine."

Sam! I blink and wipe my eyes. His face is red. His hair

is singed. And there is blood flowing from his forehead. But he is smiling like a kindergarten drawing of the sun.

"Sam!" I scream, and reach my arms around his neck and hug him. Tight.

He pulls me close and his curly hair is tickling my face and the burned smell makes my stomach jump and his Michelin Man arm is squeezing me hard and I do not mind at all.

Jessica is laughing and crying at the same time and joins our hug. I press my head against hers and both of our heads are gulping, breathing, wheezing, crying, laughing, and I do not know where her head ends and mine begins, as if she is a part of me and I am a part of her.

Rory is saying "Saaaaam" over and over.

I pull him into the hug, too, so he is surrounded by us and he is safe and we are all gasping with the same breath.

"Ma'am, you need to back away," the paramedics say. "You need to let go."

"No!" I shout. It sounds like a mighty rumble that rises from deep inside of me and breaks through my soul.

The paramedics step back but still hover around us, trying to get to Sam. They do not look happy. I do not care. I am not letting go of Sam.

There are police now, behind the paramedics. "Did anyone see who did this?"

"No," a woman's voice says. "They got away."

I hear Jessica's sob and I stand up, but I am still holding on to Sam's hand. "I can tell you what happened." It comes out loud and powerful. It is exactly how I mean it to be.

Everyone turns to look at me, the police officers, the paramedics, the people from Meeting—Phyllis is there, and

Chuck and Laurie, and the lady who called me "dear" at the last Meeting I went to—and I see other faces I know, too. My heart is pounding and I can hear my breathing but I hold my head up because there is no need to cower anymore. I have faced the Beast and his power over me is gone. I am the one with the strong spirit.

I look around the Meeting House at the expressions on each face—questioning, worried, surprised, sympathetic, kind, proud. I do not even mind being in the spotlight. "I will tell you everything," I say, my voice sounding thunderous in the silent room. "He will not hurt anyone again. It is over."

Sam squeezes my hand and I look at him. He is smiling through his burned face and I smile, squeezing his hand, too. I reach out my other hand to Jessica and she grabs it, sniffing back her tears. And I realize I am crying also. But I am crying for everything that went before, all the pain that used to be.

Rory's eyes shine up at me from Jessica's lap. "Maa—? Tay?"

I look from Rory to Jessica to Sam, and I nod yes.

Even though I am crying I nod. "Yes!"